BEDTIME STORIES TO READ TO YOURSELF IF YOU LIKE DREAMING ABOUT STUPID THINGS

JOE GERLITZ

HARPER CASE

Harper & Case
511 Avenue of the Americas
New York, NY 10011
contact: info@harpercase.com

Library of Congress Control Number: 2009941535
ISBN: 978-0-578-25706-8 (hardcover)
       978-0-578-24957-5 (paperback)
       978-0-578-25707-5 (ebook)

Printed in the United States by the first book manufacturer to join the Green Press Initiative, using sustainable and environmentally responsible practices. FSC & Rainforest Alliance certified. 100 % recycled, 30 % post-consumer waste, acid-free paper.

A SPECIAL NOTE

What you're about to read is a collection of short stories penned by a writer.

But, really, what is a writer?

Is it a person who takes a rocket into outer space? No, that's an astronaut.

Is it a person who knows how to tame tigers? No, that's a tiger tamer.

Is it a person who cobbles shoes? No, that's a cobbler.

Is it a person who takes a rocket into outer space? No, we already covered that. That person is an astronaut.

So, what is a writer?

Maybe we'll never know. Or maybe we will.

The choice is yours.

SOCCER TEAM

*L*ynn poured her husband, Jason, a cup of coffee in their newly remodeled kitchen. They'd always wanted an open floor plan and both of them loved the way it had turned out.

"I think we should encourage Travis to join a soccer team," said Lynn, cupping her coffee mug with two hands.

"A stalker team?" Jason asked. "Are you kidding me? What kind of message do you think that would be sending our son if we let him join a stalker team? So, every day after school, he's going to meet up with other stalkers and follow people around and peer into their windows and give them the creeps? Lynn, what if he takes the stalking to the next level and starts incorporating violence? What if he kills someone, Lynn?! Stalkers have been known to kill before! Join a stalker team? I can't believe you. I really can't believe you right now. You're a horrible human being. To be honest, I've always felt that way. I stopped loving you years ago."

"I actually said he should join a *soccer* team," said Lynn.

"Oh," replied Jason. "I thought you said a *stalker* team."

"Nope," said Lynn. "*Soccer*."

1

SMALL TOWN

*T*ex Jackson stepped off the train and let his gaze fall onto the dirty Western town that he'd call home for the next while. He'd heard many stories about Lincoln Town and wanted to experience it for himself. A blacksmith could plant himself anywhere and have a job, Tex told himself, so it might as well be here.

After getting his bags, Tex wandered down the dirt road to the saloon. He plopped onto a stool near the end and ordered a whiskey.

"Here you go, cowboy," said the bartender. "You new in town?"

"Fresh off the train," Tex replied. "This place seems a lot smaller than it looked in the pictures."

"Oh, yeah," said the bartender. "We're tiny. A real one-horse town."

"Well, I'll drink to that," said Tex, finishing his whiskey.

Tex tipped his cowboy hat to the bartender and strolled out into the blazing heat. Tired from his journey, Tex found a room at the Lincoln Town Hotel, laid on the bed and quickly fell asleep.

Hours later, Tex woke to a loud commotion out in the street. He could see that an older man had been shot outside the bank and seven or eight townsfolk had their guns pulled, ready to retaliate against whoever did this.

Tex put on his hat and quickly ran downstairs, where he was immediately confronted by a distraught woman.

"Please, sir! Help us!" she shrieked. "The bank was just robbed, and the thieves rode off less than five minutes ago!"

Tex pulled his gun and ran over to the posse that was forming.

"Which way did they go?" Tex asked one of the younger gunmen.

"They headed east! Five of them!" said the gunman.

"Well, let's saddle up the horses and get after them," exclaimed Tex.

The gunman looked at Tex with a blank expression.

"You mean 'saddle up the horse'—singular," he said.

"'Horse'? No, let's get all the horses out of the barn," said Tex. "And we need to hurry because they're getting farther away the more we talk!"

"Sir, I know you're new here, but we only have *one* horse," said the gunman. "I'm sure someone's told you we're only a one-horse town?"

Tex couldn't believe his ears.

"Wait. Literally? Literally you're only a one-horse town?"

"Yep. Her name's Smuckers. A real sweetheart," said the gunman.

"Well, one horse is better than none," thought Tex. "Let's get her out here so we can ride after those thieves."

The gunman looked down at the ground.

"We kind of have a problem there. See, there's a sign-up sheet for Smuckers. In fact, I got it right here."

He reached into his pocket and pulled out a large piece of paper.

"So," started the gunman, "right now, Smuckers is reserved by little Jenny Dickson's family for her birthday party. She has Smuckers until tomorrow evening. Then, from tomorrow until the following night, some of the women from the church have

Smuckers. They've been making a number of beautiful quilts and want to make sure they fit properly on her for when the weather turns. After that, Smuckers is available."

Tex showed mock interest, knowing the thieves would be long gone by then.

"So, we can have Smuckers in three days?" Tex asked.

"Yep," said the gunman. "Oh, wait. Johnny Jones has to go pick up some supplies at Snake Creek. That's about a five-day ride each way. So, I'm guessing we'll have Smuckers to ourselves in about two weeks. Then she'll be all ours, damn it! We'll go get those bastards who stole our money!"

As the gunman excitedly shot his gun into the air, Tex shook his head and went back to bed.

The next day, Tex would steal Smuckers from little Jenny Dickson's birthday party and go find a new place to call home.

FUNDRAISER

$\mathscr{B}$LOG ENTRY #1

Tomorrow, I'll begin the first leg of my journey as I attempt to pogo stick across the United States to raise money for cancer research. As many of you know, this has been a lifelong dream for me. With the help of a couple sponsors and many of you, I've already raised $35,000. I know the further I go, that number will continue to increase.

I've gotten plenty of emails asking about my plan, so let me give you a brief update. I'll be leaving on my pogo stick from Santa Monica, California, tomorrow. They're expecting a few hundred people at our kickoff ceremony. I think the mayor and a couple key fundraisers plan to say a few words. Then, two months from now, I plan to hop into the beautiful coastal city of Portland, Maine. I'm not sure what adventures await, but I know I've been training my butt off and feel like I'm in the best shape of my life. A pogo stick uses all the muscles, not just the legs. I feel like the strength I've added, along with the ridiculous cardio workouts I've put myself through, will help get me across this great country of ours and allow me to reach my goal.

I plan to blog every evening from my hotel room to give you updates on how the trip is going. I can't tell you how excited I am. I'm guessing sleep will be hard to come by tonight. Thanks, everybody!

BLOG ENTRY #2

I made it a total of six-and-a-half blocks yesterday. I'm done. This was a stupid idea. Currently at the Waffle House on Wilshire if anyone needs me.

THE ARTIST

*C*radling the brush as gently as one might a wounded sparrow, the aged artist stroked the canvas one final time to finish, arguably, his greatest masterpiece. For months he had tended to this painting, agonizing over every square inch to make sure that it would be nothing short of perfection.

Stepping back slowly, he gazed upon his completed work. Seeing it in its entirety took his breath away.

But then something caught his eye that he hadn't noticed before. The lamp in the painting was similar to the one next to him in the living room. And that chair—that chair was the exact chair just three feet from him now. The flower in the vase, the half-eaten biscuit on the plate, the straw hat—they were all in the painting exactly as they were where he stood! He then looked closer and, could it be? The man in the painting was none other than himself. This was not by choice! At no point had the artist set out to do a self-portrait.

Then the artist froze. The blood rushed from his face as his trembling hand slowly pointed to a figure standing behind him within the painting. It was a faceless man draped in black, holding a meat cleaver that reflected the brilliant full moon outside. In the painting, the faceless man was no more than five feet behind the artist. Still unable to move, the artist stood cloaked in fear. Even if he'd wanted to, his body would not have allowed him to turn around. He could not look death in the face.

Staring straight ahead, he kept his sight on the painting. A moment passed and then another image caught his eye. Behind the faceless man in the painting, there was something else. What was it? The old man's vision wasn't what it had once been, but he was now able to see clearly. Depicted behind the faceless man was a dog with its head stuck firmly inside a cooked Thanksgiving turkey. Not only that, on top of the turkey stood a chimp wearing a pirate hat, laughing and throwing large chunks of pancakes at the dog. On top of one of these pancake chunks pranced a miniature overweight mermaid holding an umbrella and wearing an Eric Dickerson jersey circa 1984.

The mesmerized artist remembered painting none of this. How was this possible? Slowly, though, the old man began to enjoy the bizarre nature of his completed painting. At first, he chuckled. And then he out-and-out laughed from deep in his belly.

It was then that the creepy guy with the meat cleaver attacked the artist and cut him up into tiny pieces.

EYE SURGERY

*D*AVE THE BIRD: Matt, it'd be great if you got your lazy eye fixed.

MATT THE BIRD: Why? I'm fine.

DAVE THE BIRD: Well, you might be fine, but the flock isn't. Every time you take the lead in our V-formation you're putting all of our lives at risk.

MATT THE BIRD: My lazy eye hasn't been that bad.

DAVE THE BIRD: 'Not that bad'? Matt, it takes us nearly three times as long to get anywhere when you're running the point because we're never flying in a straight line. Plus, last week, you led all of us directly into that wind turbine. We lost eight birds! *Good* birds!

MATT THE BIRD: You didn't have to follow me into the turbine.

DAVE THE BIRD: Of course we did! That's the whole point of the V—so that we can all chill out and not have to think about where we're going. How can we relax if our leader is veering us off course?

MATT THE BIRD: Like I said, I really don't think it's that bad.

DAVE THE BIRD: Matt, right now, I'm looking at you

and I have no idea if you're looking back at me or at that bird-seed to my right.

MATT THE BIRD: Where do you think I'm looking?

DAVE THE BIRD: The birdseed?

Matt sighs.

MATT THE BIRD: No. I was looking at you. I'll get the surgery.

LINCOLN'S FINAL WORDS

"Mary, I've never told you this, but I have a son who is not of your bloodline. His name is Chad and I'm sorry that I was unfaithful to you and I regret not telling you earlier. As you catch your breath upon hearing this shocking news, I have one more piece of information that you might find enlightening. You know the top hat that I like to wear? Of course, you do. Well, Chad has lived inside that top hat since he was a wee little infant. That's right, he just sits perched atop my head for hours on end, keeping me company and warming my head during the deathly cold months. I suppose I tell you now because Chad is no longer an infant and he's beginning to outgrow my hat. If you look closely, you can see a few of his toes poking out. Don't look too closely, of course, because Chad is painfully shy. You might think I'm breaking this news to you in the hopes that you become Chad's mother and help make a room for him in our home so that he can be part of our beautiful family. That's not the case. I only tell you this for one reason: I need a bigger hat."

Then, gunfire from Booth's pistol.

DIVORCE

"This ith one of the worth dayth of my life! How could you do thith to me?! I tried tho hard to be a good huthband, and thith ith how you repay me?! You cheat on me with my beth friend, Tham? We were going to have kidth together! Now thath all out the window! Can you thee how you hurt me tho much? I'm thorry, but I'll never forgive you! It could be theventy yearth from now and if I thee you and Tham thipping lattes at a café I'll thill hate you! I will alwayth hate you! I'm happy thith ith the end!" said Dwight, through his new Invisaligns.

WISHES

*W*hen the clock hit 2:30 every day, Eric Morgan knew exactly what he was going to do. And last Tuesday was no different.

Standing behind the cash register at IHOP, Eric stared at the pancake-shaped wall clock near the refrigerator.

2:27.

2:28.

2:29.

2:30.

Boom.

With his fifteen-minute break underway, Eric walked out the back exit with his Discman and flipped on track seven of his favorite Paula Poundstone CD. Nothing relaxed him like the art of timeless comedy.

Feeling a burst of energy, Eric decided to circle the block. There wasn't much to look at, but it still beat watching obese people with syrup stains get into their cars after a two-hour lunch.

Working at IHOP definitely wasn't Eric's life goal. Of course, that doesn't matter when you're looking at six digits in college debt while trying to support your sick grandma.

Eric turned the corner and laughed out loud at that classic line from the CD about dating. So true, Eric thought. So true.

Then something curious caught Eric's eye. Next to the fire hydrant up ahead, there was a shiny object. He'd walked this route a number of times and never noticed it.

When he got closer, he realized it was a small lamp made of gold. Eric looked around. There was no one in sight.

Because he still had twelve minutes left of his break, he picked up the lamp and examined it. It seemed like something out of a movie. The whole vibe felt very surreal.

Playing along—and kind of feeling like an idiot for doing so—Eric rubbed the lamp. He was about to set it down when, like magic, a genie appeared directly in front of him.

Eric dropped the lamp and took a few steps back.

"What the…?" said Eric.

The genie smiled.

"Don't be afraid, Eric Morgan," said the genie. "I am a genie and today has suddenly become an important one for you. Because you rubbed the magic lamp, you have been granted three wishes. These wishes can be anything you want. If you can dream it, you can wish it. So, Eric Morgan, what are your three wishes?"

Because the volume button was a bit janky on Eric's Disc-man, he still had the standup comedy blaring in his ears and was only able to hear bits and pieces of the genie's speech. Still, from what he heard, he stood there tingling with excitement.

"So, what you're telling me," he said slowly, "is that I've been granted three fishes?"

The genie quickly jumped in.

"No, no, no," the genie urgently said. "No, not three fishes. You didn't hear me correctly. No, you've been granted three —"

Eric cut him off, too overjoyed by this opportunity and still unable to completely hear the genie.

"I'll take two salmon and one cod!" Eric exclaimed.

Disheartened, the genie looked down at his shiny genie shoes.

"Wait!" Eric continued. "Can I change one of the salmon to halibut? So, one cod, one salmon and one halibut. Is it too late? Oh, man. I think I totally messed this thing up. What an idiot! I'm so sorry. Please, please, please. Can you please switch the second salmon with a halibut?"

The genie, totally bummed out, looked up.

"Yeah, I think I can do that for you," said the genie.

Unable to hear, Eric lifted up one of the headphones off his ear, Paula Poundstone still blaring.

"WHAT'D YOU SAY?" asked Eric.

The genie shook his head.

"I said," he began. "I SAID, YEAH, NO PROBLEM. I'LL MAKE THE SWITCH TO HALIBUT! IT'S LITERALLY THE LEAST I CAN DO! I'M NOT EVEN KIDDING!"

Eric was ecstatic.

"Oh my gosh," said Eric. "This is surreal. So incredible. Thank you, genie! Thank you a million times over!"

The genie disappeared.

Three fishes fell into Eric's arms.

2:45. Break was over.

A SPECIAL SURPRISE

*A*s Nick sat down in the chair near the middle of the large room, he was aware something was up. The bright lights made him squint. In the background he could see people shuffling about, prepping for something memorable. And he was smack dab in the center of it.

Nick had recently gone through a rough time. Laid off from his job as an Assistant Plant Manager at the dairy factory, Nick found comfort in his church softball team. Three games into the season, Nick strained his hamstring circling second base and would be out of commission for a few weeks.

So, when Nick's good friend, Josh, mentioned he had a little surprise that might help cheer him up, Nick had a hard time hiding his excitement. He'd seen the viral videos of critically ill medical patients being surprised in epic fashion and he thought the same kind of thing could be coming his way.

Josh sent a limo to Nick's apartment complex mid-morning to pick him up. Inside the limo were Nick's favorite breakfast items: fresh scrambled eggs, a plate of Jimmy Dean sausage and a jug of Tropicana orange juice with extra pulp. Nick devoured the feast in minutes as the limo flew down the highway.

What could my good ole pal Josh have up his sleeve,

wondered Nick. They'd met at a Great Wolf Lodge ten years ago. Josh was there with his family. Nick, alone.

The limo pulled into a large lot filled with hustle and bustle. Nick got out, brushed off a couple specks of Jimmy Dean from his chin, and was quickly escorted to the chair in the room where he now sat.

After much commotion, things calmed down and he heard a voice behind one of the large cameras that was capturing the moment in the room.

"Nick, you're probably wondering what you're doing and why you're here," said the voice.

Nick, still squinting, said, "I sure am!"

The voice stepped out from behind the camera and it was a young producer wearing a leather jacket.

"Well, my name's Tim," he said. "And we know you've gone through kind of a rough time lately."

Nick nodded his head and touched his sore hamstring. "Yep, that's right."

Tim continued. "And we also know you're about as big of a Tom Hanks fan as there is," he said.

Nick laughed.

"Yeah, no kidding! I love Tom Hanks!" said Nick.

Tim said, "Well, why don't you tell us a little about your love of Tom Hanks. What do you like about him? What are your favorite movies of his?"

Nick's pulse quickened. He was most definitely a huge Tom Hanks fan. He could now kind of see where this might be going, and he couldn't contain his enthusiasm.

"Tom Hanks is just…The Man," Nick said with a laugh. The rest of the room laughed with him. "He's simply a shining light. You know the phrase 'the girl next door'? Well, Tom gives off the vibe of the GUY next door. Just a likable gentleman who has provided some amazing performances over the years."

"Talk to us about those performances, Nick," said Tim.

Now that his eyes had finally adjusted to the brightness of

the lights, Nick could see someone standing near Tim, hidden behind the camera. In fact, it looked like this individual was wearing an obvious disguise. Collar turned up to hide the face, hat pulled down very far. Maybe even in a wig?

Nick couldn't believe what was happening.

"Um, well, Tom has been brilliant in so many films," said Nick, not taking his eyes off the hidden figure wearing the disguise. "*Saving Private Ryan*. Incredible. *Cast Away*, *Philadelphia*, *Turner & Hooch*. Oh, *Big*! I watch *Big* all the time. The dancing on the piano scene is still one of my all-time favorites. Tom Hanks is simply the best. Shoot, I could watch him eat a bowl of cereal and it'd probably be fascinating."

At this point, Nick could barely sit still in his seat.

Tim paused, allowing the excitement of the moment to build. There was an undeniable buzz in the room.

"Well," Tim said slowly, "again, we know you've had a rough go of it recently. And your good friend Josh here thought it might be fun to do something that would put a smile on your face."

Josh was now standing closer to Tim and the person in disguise had moved out of the shadow of the camera. Nick involuntarily stood up with excitement.

"So, without further ado," said Tim. "Because you obviously love Tom Hanks, we thought you might want to meet someone."

With this, Tim turned to the person in disguise. Nick took a step forward as the hat and wig began to be removed.

"Nick," said Tim. "I'd like for you to meet a close friend of mine. Mr. Greg Clemons."

With the disguise fully removed, Nick was now looking at a 65-year-old man with bad posture. Whose name was Greg.

Greg wore a Wilson The Volleyball t-shirt with the famous red handprint on it.

"Like you, Greg is a huge Tom Hanks fan," said Tim. "So, we all thought it might be super exciting for you to sit down with him and discuss all things Tom Hanks! We even got you guys a meat and cheese platter in the shape of the golden retriever from *You've Got Mail!* What do you think of that?!"

It's still unclear whether Nick intentionally pushed over the lights on his way out or if it was only an accident, but sparks flew and glass shattered as he hustled out the door.

He also strained his other hamstring, meaning it'd be at least another month before he could play church softball again.

Meanwhile, Greg tiptoed over to the snack table and tossed a couple fistfuls of gouda into his sweaty gym bag before departing.

THE RIGHT WORDS

*K*evin slumped at the dining room table with a high ball glass filled with his fourth Jim Beam of the night. Wheel of Fortune played in the background.

Kevin, eyes blurry, glanced at the TV.

The category was Place and the word was five letters long.

"I'd like to solve the puzzle, Pat," mumbled Kevin. "The answer is 'Who is Pete Sampras?'"

Kevin took another swig of his drink. He had such a close relationship with liquor these days he called Jim Beam "Jimmy Beamie". Kevin was the only one who thought the nickname was cute.

Karen Adams walked her Dalmatian past Kevin's house. Karen's insomnia made her 1 a.m. strolls a routine. She gave a small wave to Kevin from the sidewalk. Kevin returned the sentiment by tilting a cannister of Pringles in her direction.

For the last few months, Kevin had been in a rut. Once a gentle soul, he'd become ornery. Just last week, he angrily bashed in a mailbox with a baseball bat on his drive home. It wasn't until he pulled out of his driveway the next morning that he realized the mailbox was his.

This downward spiral began when Kevin's sister, Jeanie, broke her leg in a skiing accident. Kevin loved his sister. They'd been best friends growing up. Like most young siblings, they loved dressing up as characters from *Murphy Brown* and reenacting their favorite scenes. Kevin could still hear Jeanie yell, "Shut up, Miles!" as the two of them laughed themselves into hysterics.

But then she broke her leg and it crushed Kevin's soul. He had no way to console her. No words that could heal her tibia. The only thing Kevin could think of to say was, "No more ouchie now."

No more ouchie now. No more ouchie now. No more ouchie now.

As Kevin took another swig of Jimmy Beamie, he knew those words weren't enough. 'No more ouchie now'? What the heck did that even mean? Kevin stood up so violently, his chair tipped over. He reared back and threw his glass against the wall. It exploded, sending tiny shards everywhere. He let out a barbaric scream that both Karen and her Dalmatian could hear from a block away.

Though he was in no shape to drive, Kevin grabbed the keys to his Outback and stumbled down the front stairs. On evenings like this, home felt like prison. Besides, he was craving grocery store fried chicken.

He got behind the wheel with Jimmy Beamie in his bloodstream and tears in his eyes.

No more ouchie now.

No more ouchie now.

Shut up, Miles!

Somehow, Kevin made it safely to the grocery store. The only employee at checkout recognized Kevin and simply rolled his eyes.

Kevin knew the quickest way to the fried chicken was aisle 7. Even with his blurred vision, he could see the heat lamps in the back of the store keeping yesterday's chicken nice and crispy.

No more ouchie now.

No more ouchie now.

No more—

Something caught his attention. It was the greeting card section. He turned and dropped to his knees, tears immediately streaming down his cheeks.

GET. WELL. SOON.

Finally.

Those were the words his beloved sister needed to hear. Somehow, a poet took his 'no more ouchie now' sentiment and turned it into a language all its own. It was so personal. So expressive. And it had an image of a penguin holding a thermometer.

Minutes later, Kevin would sit down in the middle of aisle 7 in his freshly soiled pants, eating day-old fried chicken and reading the message over and over that he'd spent weeks trying to communicate himself.

Get well soon.

IMMATURE SQUIRREL

A mother squirrel and a father squirrel sat at the dinner table eating walnuts with their son. Unlike most evenings, the mood was quite tense.

"I have something to tell you, Son," said the father squirrel. "While it grieves me to say this, you should know that your mother and I are getting separated. Right now, we don't know exactly what this means. Neither of us wants a divorce, so we're going to do everything in our power to work on our marriage during this separation. This in no way is because of you, Son. We both love you very, very much. We're going to continue to be the very best parents we can be, even though we're not living under the same roof. Again, we want the best for each other as well as for you."

After speaking, the father squirrel, exhausted, leaned back in his chair. The mother squirrel dabbed her watery eyes with a handkerchief. Both parents sat quietly as their son processed this life-altering news.

The son finally spoke.

"Hey, Dad," the son said. "Your nuts are showing. Get it? Nuts! Hahaha."

The father squirrel sighed while the mother squirrel began to do the dishes.

That evening, while his wife and son slept, the father squirrel traveled to Las Vegas, where he auditioned for Zumanity, Cirque du Soleil's burlesque show that, according to the brochure, "raises temperatures underneath the big top." He didn't get the part and his current whereabouts remain unknown.

WEDDING VOWS

*G*ROOM: I take you, Natalie, to be my wife.

BRIDE: I take you, John, to be my husband.

GROOM: I promise to love you until death do us part.

BRIDE: I promise to love you until death do us part.

GROOM: I will always care for you in sickness and in health, and never consider putting a ninja move on you while you sleep.

BRIDE: I will always care for you in sickness and in health.

GROOM: My devotion will always be to you and I will resist all temptation to lower myself from the ceiling in a super-stealth way and do a ninja move on you.

BRIDE: My devotion will always be to you.

GROOM: For better and for worse, I will always remain by your side. And will fight the urges deep within me to try out some of those new crazy-sweet ninja moves on you, like hiding behind your car seat and suddenly swinging my legs upward and snapping your neck with a classic scissor technique.

BRIDE: For better and for worse, I will always remain by your side.

OFFICIANT: I now pronounce you Man and Wife.

Epilogue: Two months after the honeymoon, Natalie died. You'd probably guess it was from a ninja move. But it was actually from a heart attack.

ICED TEA

*E*van left his apartment for the first time in a few days. It's nearly impossible to describe how bad Evan smelled.

He was only fifteen pounds overweight but smelled like someone three times his size. The smell was like a mixture of an undercooked salmon that was left on a kitchen counter for five days and another undercooked salmon that was left on a kitchen counter for five days. So, in total, two undercooked salmon. It was like he just played a three-hour pickup basketball game against a team of wet dogs. When he lifted his arms to give a high five or to hang curtains, you'd look around for a corpse. It was like his whole body had bad breath. If he were sitting in a chair and someone dumped a bowl of cooked onions onto the chair next to him, no one would notice. In fact, some might say the smell just improved. Twice, raccoons have climbed on top of him while he slept and tried to pry his pajamas open, thinking he was a garbage can full of discarded pork chops and spoiled yogurt. The closest he'd come to going on a date was fifty feet. As in, the girl got within fifty feet of him, fought off a gag reflex for around 20-25 seconds, then caught an Uber and had the driver go fast in the other direction. She ended up vomiting inside the car.

Anyway, Evan grabbed an iced tea from the nearby convenience store and returned to his apartment.

PLANE CRASH

*T*his is an inner dialogue absolutely no one would have with themselves if the airplane they were riding in was plummeting to Earth in a fiery ball.

30,000 feet: *I can't believe the plane has partially exploded and we're all going to be dead pretty soon.*

25,000 feet: *I hope I left my TV on a really cool channel in case anyone comes into my home after I die and turns it on. If it's set to the Lifetime network, I'll be totally embarrassed.*

20,000 feet: *Why do they call a mini-fridge a 'mini-fridge'? It's not like it's a miniature version of a fridge. Oh, actually, it is. I take that back.*

15,000 feet: *I wish at some point in my life, I had tried parting my hair on the left instead of the right. Not my head hair. My chest hair.*

10,000 feet: *That screaming gal across the aisle is pretty cute. Maybe I'll ask her out. I'd like for her to meet my parents. Maybe we could all go out for Thai food sometime. Oh, that's right. Our plane is going to crash.*

5,000 feet: *Greg. Marsha. Cindy. Jan. Peter. Who was the*

youngest Brady boy? Gosh, Alice really loved bowling now that I think about it.

1,000 feet: *I assume they're not going to bring the beverage cart around one more time. But I'm not sure of it.*

500 feet: *I wonder if it's too late to order the U.S. Cavalry replica sword out of this SkyMall magazine.*

300 feet: *What is this? A mustard stain on my jeans? I just bought these jeans. Wait. It's just a piece of yellow lint. It really looked like a mustard stain for a minute there. Makes sense, since I don't remember eating anything with mustard recently.*

100 feet: *'Get 'er done'...I wonder who came up with that phrase. It's pretty funny.*

5 feet: *I'm bored.*

SOUP RECIPE

Some people are blessed to have mothers, grandmothers and even great-grandmothers who love cooking and have countless recipes to share. These recipes become heirlooms and tell an even deeper story than a simple family tree ever could.

The following is one such recipe, passed down from generation to generation. Bon appétit!

½ tsp salt
¼ tsp pepper
6 medium carrots
1 cup peas
2 cans beef broth
3 medium potatoes
1 tsp ground mustard
1 can tomato sauce
1 Shetland pony*

*It's preferable that the Shetland pony has a state fair or carnival background. This type of constant activity will mean that the animal—and, therefore, the meat—will be more lean. A Shetland pony that only grazes will have more fat. Also, a carnival Shetland pony tends to be happier and that's a difference you can taste. Before grinding up the entire Shetland pony in the food processor (3 hours on High), feel free to remove the hooves. They make great ashtrays for the gals!

TRANSCRIPT FROM A NASCAR RACE

1:07 PM—Crew Chief: "Okay, Max. The race just started, so you're gonna want to step on the gas pedal."

1:08 PM—Crew Chief: "Max, you're going to have a left turn coming up."

1:09 PM—Crew Chief: "A little heads-up, Max. You're going to have another left turn coming up."

1:10 PM—Crew Chief: "Good left turning, Max."

1:11 PM—Crew Chief: "Don't forget to press on the gas pedal with your foot, Max. I can't stress this enough. We all agree."

1:12 PM—Crew Chief: "Got another left turn coming up, Max."

1:13 PM—Crew Chief: "In a short bit, you're going to have another left turn."

1:14 PM—Crew Chief: "Nice job stepping on the gas pedal, Max."

1:15 PM—Crew Chief: "Hey, Max. Frank wanted me to tell you something. That piece of information is that there's a left turn on the horizon."

1:16 PM—Crew Chief: "Max, dynamite job out there. Just keep remembering to step on the gas pedal and not the brake pedal."

1:17 PM—Crew Chief: "Okay, you're in a part of the track right now where you need to keep pressing your foot on the gas pedal. Perfect."

1:18 PM—Crew Chief: "If you haven't noticed, there are a lot of cars around you. Don't freak out."

1:19 PM—Crew Chief: "Got a left turn here."

1:20 PM—Crew Chief: "Another left turn here."

1:21 PM—Crew Chief: "Okay, Max, you're gonna want to take a right turn here. Wait! I'm sorry. A left turn. I was reading the map wrong."

HELP WANTED

*A*TTENTION: FIRE TRUCK DRIVER NEEDED
Fire Station #16 in Oakland, CA is in need of
someone who will safely and effectively drive the station's fire
truck during emergencies. Driver should have at least five years
of experience. Must provide three references.

Also, if called upon during a 4-alarm fire in the Grand
Lake area, it's preferred that the driver doesn't accidentally pull
forward and park on top of the hose and then hop out of the
truck with the keys locked inside, making it impossible to get
water through the hose. Costing the lives of seven residents,
two firefighters and the entire city block. And disgracing our
entire station.

And if the occasion happens to arise in which there's a 3-
alarm fire in Adams Point, as a general rule of thumb please
don't feel that "stopping real quick" at a DQ drive-thru for a
Blizzard is an option.

Finally, if you're going to switch the traditional fire truck
siren to Glenn Frey's "The Heat Is On" as a joke without
telling anyone, please reconsider.

Reply to this post or call the number below if interested.

Mikey Gunderson. The previous driver's name was Mikey
Gunderson.

TIME TRAVEL

$\mathcal{W}$ith both a hint of excitement and trepidation, Marc and Aaron approached the large, mysterious object covered with a sheet of canvas. They knew they weren't supposed to be in this tucked-away, archived section of the university, but they were in the mood for a little exploration and somehow they'd ended up here.

From its giant bulky shape, they could tell the covered item wasn't a normal piece of school equipment. Around them were old beakers, microscopes and other things used in the science lab at some point during the university's 130-year history.

But this item was different.

They pulled back the dusty, draped canvas, moving quickly in their eagerness to see what was hidden. Seconds later, they were looking at a large machine in front of them. They glanced curiously at each other, wondering what it could be. Then Aaron noticed a note attached.

He read it aloud: "Dear Fellow Explorer. Congratulations. You have just discovered the time-travel machine I've spent my entire life creating. With this machine, you'll be able to travel anywhere, be it in the past or in the future. Just type in the date and place of your desired destination and you'll be transported there in an instant. This is my gift to you. Signed, Professor Stanley."

Marc and Aaron stared at each other wide-eyed. Dr. Stanley was a well-known science professor who had passed away nearly ten years ago. He had always been working on experiments that were either illegal or simply unorthodox. There had been rumors of this so-called time machine, but no one had ever seen it.

"Do you know what this means?" asked Marc. "We can go anywhere and any place we want. This might be the greatest invention ever. And it's all ours."

"Do you think it's real?" asked Aaron. "Like, do you think it ...works?"

Marc laughed.

"Well, there's only one way to find out. This is our opportunity to be a part of something amazing. We can go anywhere, at any point in history. This is our chance to dream. So, my new time-traveling pal, where should we go first?"

Aaron thought for a little bit. Finally, a light went on in his head and he looked at Marc.

"Hey, remember how curious and excited we were two minutes ago when we didn't know what was under the canvas?" he asked. "Well, let's travel back in time and relive that moment."

Marc shook his head.

"What, are you an idiot?" said Marc. "We can go anywhere in the world at any time, and you want to travel back two minutes? I was thinking we go back at least five minutes. That's when our curiosity was the highest."

"Yeah," said Aaron. "You're totally right. Let's do this."

Aaron and Marc leaped into the time machine, buckled up and typed in the day's date. They hit the red "Explore" button and held on for dear life.

They were instantly transported five minutes back in time. Same room, but about ten feet from where they'd just been. The two friends hopped out of the time machine.

"Whoa!" exclaimed Marc. "That was incredible! Look at where we are! This is amazing!"

Aaron was jumping up and down.

"This is the greatest adventure I've ever heard of!" he said. "Just think of all the other possibilities for our time-traveling!"

"I know," said Marc. "I've got an insane idea for our next destination. What if we did one minute from now in the future, still in this room? It's like fast-forwarding us a little bit so that we'd be four minutes in the past from where we initially traveled from."

"Let's do it!" exclaimed Aaron.

The pair quickly jumped back in the time machine, buckled up, set the time for one minute in the future and punched the button. They immediately moved four feet and one minute ahead in the future. The two rolled out of the capsule, laughing and high fiving.

"We are real time travelers!" said Aaron.

"I know!" replied Marc. "Think about this, Aaron. The possibilities are limitless. We can go anywhere and experience anything firsthand. If we wanted, we could travel back in time like, say, ten minutes. Remember that? We were walking across the quad. We could go right back there! Or imagine going twenty minutes into the future! What will our world look like then? What types of civilizations will live on our planet? Will there even be an 'our planet'? We can report back all of our findings to everyone when we return."

Aaron nodded along.

"Or what if we traveled way back in time? Like, a half-hour," said Aaron. "I was eating a corn dog for lunch and you were enjoying a delicious-looking casserole. How incredible would that be? How surreal would that be for you to eat the same casserole for lunch?"

Marc was already climbing back into the time machine before Aaron could finish his sentence.

"Of course," Marc said, "You know that means I'll have to

eat my second dessert of the day, right? With all of this time traveling, I hope I don't get fat!"

The two laughed long and hard, stopping only to catch their breath.

Because they were morons.

WHAT ADAM AND EVE BICKERED ABOUT

1. Adam never helping Eve pull weeds in the Garden of Eden.
2. Eve complaining that they never go on double dates.
3. Adam blaming Eve for his misplaced car keys, sparking a bigger argument about what a car is.
4. After being away for a while, Eve suspiciously telling Adam that she had gone to see a movie.
5. Adam making the 'What is this, a nudist colony?' joke way too often.
6. Eve not being sure she wanted to have kids, prompting Adam to remind her that if they didn't, the human race would end.
7. Adam being allergic to most plants and flowers.
8. Adam always trying to find a way to drop the 'says the chick who ate the forbidden fruit' line on Eve.
9. Being constantly confused about whether the dinosaurs had already existed or if they were still on their way.
10. Eve getting tired of Adam always bragging that he's the greatest runner ever, the greatest speller ever, the greatest climber ever, etc.

GOLDILOCKS, HER LOSER BOYFRIEND CRAIG AND THE 3 BEARS

*O*nce upon a time, there was a little girl named Goldilocks. She went for a walk in the forest. Pretty soon, she came upon a house. She knocked and, when no one answered, she walked right in.

Oh, and she brought her loser boyfriend, Craig, with her.

At the table in the kitchen, there were three bowls of porridge. Goldilocks was hungry. She tasted the porridge from the first bowl.

"This porridge is too hot!" she exclaimed.

So, she tasted the porridge from the second bowl.

"This porridge is too cold," she said.

So, she tasted the last bowl of porridge.

"Ahh, this porridge is just right," she said happily, and she ate it all up.

Meanwhile, Craig had opened up every cupboard in the kitchen, accidentally breaking a few plates in the process.

"Doesn't this family have any booze in the house?" asked Craig. "Some strawberry Boone's Farm? It's time to get crazy."

He then somewhat-purposefully elbowed a honey jar heirloom off the kitchen counter.

"Grow up, Craig!" shouted Goldilocks.

"YOU grow up," muttered Craig as he started fiddling with the TV remote, looking for the Detroit Red Wings game.

After she'd eaten the three bears' breakfasts, Goldilocks decided she was feeling a little tired. So, she walked into the living room where she saw three chairs. Goldilocks sat in the first chair to rest her feet.

"This chair is too big!" she exclaimed, and moved to the second chair.

"This chair is big, too!" she whined.

So, she tried the last and smallest chair.

"Ahh, this chair is just right," she sighed.

"Babe," said Craig, over by the mantle.

Goldilocks refused to look over in his direction.

"Hey, babe," said Craig. "Babe. Babe, check it out."

She finally looked over and saw that he was inching an urn containing the bears' deceased grandmother closer and closer to the edge of the mantle.

"Craig," Goldilocks said. "Don't—"

The urn tumbled off the mantle, its ashes falling everywhere. The urn hit Craig's foot, prompting him to let out a scream as he kicked it across the room.

Goldilocks shook her head and quickly hopped up from the chair and headed toward the stairs.

When she got upstairs, she saw three beds. She laid down in the first bed, but it was too hard. Then she laid down in the second bed, but it was too soft. Then she laid down in the third bed and it was just right.

But then Craig came in, having just removed his shirt. He stood in the doorway, flexing. Craig had always been good at doing that thing where you make your pecs kind of bounce by clinching your chest muscles. It was obvious he'd just done a set of twenty push-ups to look more buff.

"Hey, Goldie," said Craig. "Check out my pecs. You like that? You like how I can make my pecs bounce around like that?"

Goldilocks just rolled her eyes before turning over in bed and facing the other way.

"I bet I can do that with my butt, too, if I tried," said Craig. "Just give me a minute. Give me a minute and I'll put on a show for you, Goldie! I'll give you the show of a lifetime!"

The first swipe of Papa Bear's claw ripped off a thick layer of flesh from Craig's back.

Too shocked to scream, Craig simply turned around to see the three bears had returned: Papa Bear, Mama Bear and Baby Bear.

Papa Bear roared and took another swipe at Craig. This time he managed to take off Craig's left ear and some of his shoulder. Craig screamed in agony.

Goldilocks, completely unbothered by what was going on with Craig, saw this as an opportunity to sneak out a nearby window. She shimmied her way down a lattice fence and poured herself an extra bowl of porridge to take with her on her trip home.

Upstairs, all three bears were taking turns ripping Craig apart. Papa Bear used Craig's severed arm to wave flirtatiously to Mama Bear. Meanwhile, Baby Bear, still too young to get in on a good mauling, contributed by routinely swinging a Louisville Slugger at Craig's head.

The End.

TANDEM BICYCLISTS

*A*fter one of the greatest careers ever known in competitive tandem cycling, Ingrid Johansson and Eva Nilsson sat down for one last interview. Though they were starting to show their age at 67 and 65, respectively, the two teammates still appeared to be in excellent condition.

Lars Andersson, longtime Swedish TV host, hugged them both as they walked onto the stage. An appreciative audience gave them a standing ovation.

Soaking it all in, Ingrid and Eva finally sat down in their seats.

Lars, feeling giddier than normal because of his two celebrity guests, jumped right in with a question.

"Thank you so much for being here," said Lars. "How does one even begin to sum up the brilliant career you two have had?"

Eva chimed in first.

"What we've accomplished—and what we've experienced —over the last forty years has been nothing short of remark-able," said Eva. "Because of our hard work and dedication, we've been able to see the entire world. And I almost mean that literally!"

The audience quietly chuckled to themselves.

"Ingrid and I have cycled through the plains of Africa," Eva continued. "We've raced through the Alps too many times to count. We've competed—and won, I might add—in places like Japan and Australia and India. It's truly been an unbelievable career. And I am so honored I've been able to share it with my co-pilot and best friend, Ingrid."

With that, Eva reached over and gently touched Ingrid's arm.

Lars, clearly emotional by Eva's tribute to her riding partner, turned to Ingrid.

"So, Ingrid, I assume the feeling is mutual?" he asked.

Surprisingly, Ingrid didn't reply right away. Instead, she looked around the studio for a couple moments. Lars and Eva gave each other a confused glance.

Staring down at her feet, Ingrid finally spoke.

"You never let me ride in the front," she mumbled.

Unable to clearly hear Ingrid's words, Lars asked her to repeat what she said.

"You never let me ride in the front," said Ingrid. "For the past four decades, while you've had an unobstructed view of the greatest landmarks and creations known to mankind, I've been staring at your back. And smelling your eggy farts."

The audience gasped.

Eva touched Ingrid's arm again, but Ingrid quickly pulled away.

"Ingrid, I never—" said Eva before Ingrid cut her off.

"I'm not kidding," continued Ingrid. "How many miles do you think we've traveled together? Millions, I suppose. That's millions of miles in which all I've done is pedal hard and inhale your eggy farts. I recently saw a photo. It was of the Eiffel Tower, taken during one of our races. I immediately smelled eggy farts. Because that's how deep it is in my subconscious. It's like I have your entire butt in my mouth and I won't be able to get the taste out until I'm dead."

After letting Ingrid's comment sink in, Lars turned back to Eva, who was sobbing uncontrollably.

"So," he said. "Do you gals ride a Schwinn or...?"

BALLOON

I know that balloon is about to pop.

It's inevitable.

Whoever was in charge of hanging this particular balloon did a lousy job. It was probably Linda. And now I hate her.

Directly above the heat vent.

Near the edge of the venetian blinds.

Too close to the sill where the cat hangs out.

Not far enough out of reach from the fingernails of all the kids at this birthday party.

She could've hung this balloon anywhere. Like over there by the kitchen island. Or by the stairwell. Or above the TV.

Not there. In this location, she's begging for this balloon to be popped.

And when that happens, all hell will break loose.

Initially, every child will stop what they're doing and look up. That moment will quickly pass and what comes next will be screaming, tears, kids rushing to their parents, parents pleading with their kids to stop crying while bribing them with pacifiers and treats and asking them if it's nap time and wives painfully looking up at husbands quietly mouthing if it's time to leave and if you'll go get the car like right now I'm serious please go get it right now.

And when that happens, instead of being able to finish my beer and enjoy a piece of that Harry Potter cake, I'll be forced to go home with our crying child and will likely be told to finish trimming the shrubs.

This could've been avoided.

Damn you, Linda.

BASEBALL PITCHER

*L*ittle Nathan Darwood stood alone on the pitcher's mound and stared in at the catcher. It was his first real baseball game. Like the rest of the kids, he'd played t-ball for a season. But we all know that t-ball doesn't hold a candle to the real thing.

Nathan's parents, Thomas and Becky, sat nervously in the stands. There's a lot of pressure when your son is playing in his first baseball game, let alone pitching in it. Becky anxiously squeezed Thomas's hand hard. Because Thomas had hand surgery that very morning, it hurt really bad. But he didn't say anything to Becky and instead mentally filed it away, deciding he'd reference it the next time they had a big argument.

Besides, this day wasn't about hand surgeries and marital tension. It was about Nathan. And Nathan had a rocket for an arm. Everyone said so. For whatever reason, the kid could simply throw it harder than anyone else his age. Even Mr. Ribbons, his PE teacher at school, would wince whenever he played catch with Nathan.

Was Nathan taking hardcore steroids? Not a chance. Was he taking medium-core steroids? Probably not. 8-year-olds normally aren't into that kind of crap. There's a good chance

Nathan just happened to be born with an amazing throwing arm.

With the game ready to start, Nathan steadied himself on the mound. He rocked back, twisted his body, kicked up his leg, cocked his arm back and, with a violent tornado-like motion, fired the baseball toward home plate.

The batter, little Wes Jacobs, could only close his eyes and swing at the blur. He was four seconds late and two feet away from the intended target. Even the catcher, little Davey Ingram, had no idea where the ball was heading so he pee-peed a couple dribbles in his uniform pants as he closed his eyes and held up his mitt. He didn't come close to catching it.

Shoot, even Mr. Watkins, the volunteer umpire who'd been clean from his meth habit for six years, couldn't see it and decided to crouch out of harm's way.

The baseball hit the backstop and, with the sound of gunfire, split one of the wood boards in two. Surprisingly, the backstop did nothing to slow down the velocity or trajectory of Nathan's thrown baseball.

Mr. and Mrs. Nelson's Dodge Durango, parked on the street fifteen feet from the playfield, was the next victim. The baseball shot through the back window before completely shattering the front windshield. Again, the baseball didn't slow down.

Nathan's pitch ended up busting through a couple restaurant windows, knocking over a few indigenous trees, crossing a bunch of state lines, going over one ocean before finally rolling to a stop next to a hut in Zaire, midway through a beautiful tribal dance. A baby might've glanced over but, for the most part, no one really even noticed it.

And that's when Mr. Watkins, the volunteer umpire who'd been clean from his meth habit for six years, stood up from his crouch back at the original baseball field and said, "Striiiiiiike one!"

And the whole world laughed. Even the Zairnese or whatever they're called.

LARRY THE CAT

*A*s Daniel placed the newspaper on the coffee table and prepared to hop in the shower, he gave a quick look to his large Persian cat, Larry, who had been nuzzled next to him.

"Hi, Lair-Lair," said Daniel, patting him on the head.

"Good morning, Daniel," said Larry.

A couple things stood out to Daniel at this very moment. The first was that his cat just talked. The second was that he didn't know his cat could talk.

Daniel sat back down.

He looked deeply into Larry's eyes, searching for some kind of clue pertaining to what just happened. His search turned up empty. Instead, it was Larry who once again initiated contact.

Larry held up his paw and said, "Hold on. Give me one sec."

Daniel then watched in disbelief as Larry used his furry, fumbling paws to unzip what he could now see was actually a miniature suit made of fur and whiskers. Once the suit was fully unzipped, what remained was a tiny man, probably no older than 58, slightly overweight. He was sweating quite manically from the fur.

Once he wiped off the sweat from his body, he extended that sweaty hand in Daniel's direction.

"Sorry about all that," he said. "How are you doin', Daniel? I'm Ted."

Daniel hesitated for quite a while, until he begrudgingly extended his hand.

"Hi...Ted," whispered Daniel.

The two just looked at each other.

"What are you doing here, Ted?" asked Daniel.

"Here as in the living room?" replied Ted.

"Nope," replied Daniel. "Not even close to what I was asking. I know why you're in the living room. You were here snuggling into me as I read the newspaper. What I'm now wondering, as if I have to spell it out, is why my cat is actually a miniature person in a cat suit."

Ted nodded, now understanding the true source of Daniel's confusion.

"I suggest you ask Ms. Lithington," said Ted.

Daniel just stared at Ted, so Ted continued.

"Here's the deal. See, about five years ago, I took some night classes at Shoreline Community College. I'd been working as an assistant store manager of Ladies Foot Locker for almost a decade and dang it if I wasn't tired of women's athletic shoes and craving something different! So, I decided to become an actor. Ms. Lithington was my teacher. An eccentric type. A total wack job actually. And she encouraged her students to really get into their studies. 'Go extreme', she would always say. On one particular assignment, I had mentioned to her about the cat suit. She loved it. So, knowing that your wife is a cat lover, I hung out and meowed outside your apartment door until she invited me in. I've been acting like a cat ever since."

Daniel, clearly uncomfortable by all this, moved even further away on the couch.

"But," started Daniel, "you say that was five years ago. Isn't that class over and done with?"

"Oh, 100%," said Ted. "But I couldn't care less about that class now. I'm happy here. Your wife loves me. You're good about keeping my litter box clean. I've found a home, Daniel."

Daniel fiddled with a drink coaster.

"Ted," said Daniel, "I don't mean to be rude here—and I *do* appreciate your forthrightness, don't get me wrong—but you eat our food, you scratch up our furniture. Ted, now that I think about it, you always sit at the end of the bed and watch as my wife and I make love. It all just seems a little weird to me."

Ted leaned in as closely as Daniel would allow him.

"I understand your feelings, Daniel," said Ted. "But I encourage you to consider all the ways I've made your life better. How I usually greet you at the door after work. How I give you a nuzzle when I know you need it the most. The way I—"

"Sorry to cut you off, Ted," said Daniel. "But I'm just now thinking about how you lick your butthole after going to the bathroom."

Ted slumped, embarrassed.

"I'd rather not talk about that," said Ted. "I guess, Daniel, my point is that I've always felt our relationship—you, me, Teri—has always been extremely reciprocal. Classic give-and-take."

"Does Teri know about this?" asked Daniel.

Ted shook his head.

"No," he replied. "It would crush her. We have an unbelievable relationship right now and I don't want that to change. She'd probably toss me out into the street. Or withhold Fancy Feast from me. Either way, I don't want to risk it."

Daniel and Ted sat in awkward silence. Daniel noticed Ted glancing at the Showcase Showdown on *The Price Is Right*. He could see Ted trying to figure out how much the jet skis were worth.

"Coughing up hairballs has to hurt," said Daniel.

Ted laughed and slapped Daniel on the knee.

"You wouldn't believe the discomfort!" exclaimed Ted, hand still resting on Daniel's knee.

A moment passed and then they both heard Teri's key in the door.

"See ya, Dan," said Ted.

"Bye, Ted," said Daniel.

Ted quickly zipped up his cat suit. He wandered off to find Teri's legs.

"Hiya, Lair-Lair," said Teri.

THE FIRST HIGH FIVE

*D*onald Tilson stood near midcourt with his left hand extended into the air.

His team, Jefferson High School, had just won the 1916 Indiana State Championship by defeating Crawfordsville High. Tilson was responsible for scoring the only basket in overtime, clinching the win for Jefferson.

And now he stood facing his teammate Ray Campbell, hand raised, brimming with victorious enthusiasm.

But Donald's actions caused great confusion.

And, slowly, a gentle hush fell over the packed gymnasium.

Mr. Garrett, the former opium addict who ran the local general store, was the first to speak up.

"Donald's hand is raised! This must mean he has a pressing question that he'd like answered!" shouted Mr. Garrett.

From the other side of the gymnasium came another voice. This time from Marjorie Timmons, science teacher at Crawfordsville.

"His question is probably about the Titanic!" Marjorie shouted. "You remember the Titanic?! The big boat that sank a couple years ago?! He's probably wondering how many people perished!"

Donald continued standing there, hand in the air.

Again, another voice pierced the silence.

"From what I hear, more than a thousand people perished!" yelled Sam McGee, a top salesman in the Lafayette area. "Maybe even 1,500! So, if Donald is raising his hand right now because he has a question about how many people perished on the Titanic, it was around 1,500!"

Another voice. This time from Carol Meyer, a local florist.

"But what if his question isn't about the Titanic at all?" Carol yelled. "What if it's about this Great Depression we've been hearing so much about?!"

Skippy Dolittle, a writer for the *Indianapolis Star*, responded.

"The Great Depression is definitely looming!" shouted Dolittle. "If you ask me, the whole thing sounds depressing!"

"No one asked you!" yelled Marjorie Timmons.

Again, the gymnasium fell silent. All eyes remained transfixed on midcourt where Donald Tilson continued to stand with his hand raised.

After a few moments, Donald finally addressed the crowd.

"I don't have a question!" Donald shouted, hand still up in the air. "I'm just happy our team won the basketball game and I want to give my teammate, Ray, a Five Finger Slappy!"

Upon hearing this, a curious buzz filled the gym.

A "Five Finger Slappy"? What was a "Five Finger Slappy"? More importantly, did Ray Campbell know what it was, and was he willing to accept?"

So many questions.

Ultimately, Ray slowly raised his own hand in the air. Like only two in-sync teammates can, the players each took a step toward the other person and — smack! —slapped their hands together.

It was nothing like anyone had ever seen before.

Mr. Garrett had to ruin the significant moment with another interjection.

"Hey!" shouted Mr. Garrett. "Since both your hands were high in the air, why not call it a High Five?!"

Donald and Ray were nearly to the locker room doors by this point. But before they disappeared, Donald responded.

"Nope!" Donald yelled. "We're going with 'Five Finger Slappy'!"

The two players continued jogging into the locker room.

Ten minutes later, Donald returned to the court and said that "High Five" was probably a better name and, moving forward, everyone should just call it that.

The crowd went absolutely nuts.

Lost in all the hubbub was that, standing courtside that very night as a Jefferson High cheerleader, was none other than sixteen-year-old Agnes Moorehead, who would later go on to play Endora on *Bewitched*.

Her and Donald ended up fooling around in the parking lot after the game.

Just over-the-clothes stuff.

WRITER'S BLOCK

For hours, Devin stared at the computer screen. The blank page with the blinking cursor both mesmerized and troubled him. He put his head in his hands and glanced down at his feet. A squawking crow outside caught his attention. But just as quickly as the crow appeared, it departed. Devin turned his eyes back to the computer.

Again, the blinking cursor.

Again, the empty page.

Again, the silence.

Devin then vomited carrots all over the monitor while at the same time crapping his pants. Because he was 9 months old.

BEARD CONTEST

*W*ith the beard-growing championship just a week away, friends Pete and Brent met for lunch to track each other's progress. The two looked at the menu. Pete was in the mood for a calzone, while Brent had his eye on the Cobb salad.

"I notice your beard looks rich and full," said Pete.

"Yes, it's coming in nicely," said Brent.

The two watched as a family entered the restaurant and sat in a nearby booth. The youngest kid looked like a total brat.

"By the same token," Brent continued. "I can't help but notice your face is void of all hair."

Pete nodded.

"Yep, it's been very frustrating," he said. "After I got done shaving this morning, I became depressed about how little my beard has grown in."

Brent looked up from the menu.

"Pete, you mentioned you shaved this morning," said Brent. "I'm not an expert, but do you think that could have anything to do with your inability to grow a beard?"

Pete waved him off.

"Get real," Pete said.

"Pete, I'm just looking at the facts and doing the math

right now and I feel like the shaving aspect is a key ingredient that's holding you back from growing a beard," said Brent.

"There's no way," Pete said. "In fact, yesterday, after I had my weekly face wax, I sat down on a bench in Gilmore Park and decided I haven't been growing a good beard because I haven't been applying myself."

Once again, Brent gave a confused expression.

"Pete, you just mentioned something that I feel could be another reason for your inability to grow a beard," said Brent.

"The part about the bench-sitting?" asked Pete.

"No," said Brent. "The part about you getting your face waxed. I've got to think that the face waxing, in addition to the shaving, is really preventing you from growing a beard. I mainly feel this way because—and please don't think that I'm judging you—by doing those two things, you're actually removing facial hair as opposed to giving your facial hair a chance to grow."

Pete grew upset.

"Brent, just because some of us weren't born with a silver spoon on our face doesn't mean we can't grow a good beard. Something just isn't working right now. Eventually, it'll click. I know it will, Brent. I know it will click!"

Epilogue: You might remember the story about Brent and Pete and the facial hair thing. Anyway, it never "clicked" for Pete.

WISDOM

*C*aleb sat outside on his favorite deck chair, holding a hot coffee and reflecting on the incredible amount of wisdom he'd gained from his life experiences thus far. Like so many others in their early forties, it was easy to look back and reconsider all the choices he'd made. If only I could go back in time and talk some sense into my younger self, he often thought. If Caleb could do that maybe, just maybe, things would've turned out differently.

As Caleb took another sip of coffee, he thought even more about what he'd say to his younger self. And he decided that this is how that conversation would go…

CURRENT CALEB: Hi, there. Can I talk to you for a little bit?

YOUNGER CALEB: Who the hell are you? How'd you get in my room?

CURRENT CALEB: Don't be scared. I'm you, 25 years from now.

YOUNGER CALEB: Did you just kill my parents? Where are my parents?

CURRENT CALEB: Oh, you mean Gordon and Judy? They're my parents, too. No, I'm sure they're fine. I just wanted to talk to you about our life.

YOUNGER CALEB: Get out of here! I'm not kidding!

CURRENT CALEB: Whoa, calm down. I want to impart some wisdom that you can take with you as you grow up.

YOUNGER CALEB: THERE'S A MAN IN MY ROOM AND HE'S GOING TO KILL ME! SOMEONE PLEASE HELP! IF YOU CAN HEAR ME, CALL THE POLICE! I DON'T WANT TO DIE! I DON'T WANT TO DIE!

CURRENT CALEB: Okay. Hey, I'll leave now. Oh, before I go, give Angela Thompson a fair shake. She gets a lot hotter after high school.

YOUNGER CALEB: LEAVE NOW!!!

CURRENT CALEB: Last thing! Despite Ellen DeGeneres's indelible performance as Bill Pullman's love interest in the 1996 comedy, *Mr. Wrong*, it turns out she's gay.

YOUNGER CALEB: If she's gay, then that makes Bill Pullman a lesbian as well. Because those two had me convinced the love they shared was real!

SPORTS FANS

*B*eing careful to avoid hitting other sports fans, Paul drove slowly down the tree-lined street just four blocks from the stadium.

"There's a spot," shouted Doug from the backseat.

"That's a really good one, Paul," said Steve. "So close to the stadium. You gotta take this!"

Paul examined the spot for a moment and sized up the space against the length of his Corolla.

"I don't know, guys," he said. "Looks pretty tight."

The friends in the backseat gave Paul shouts of encouragement.

"Oh, you got this!"

"I've seen you fit in smaller parking spaces than this, Paul!"

"All you, baby. All you."

Paul briefly closed his eyes, composed himself and began turning the wheel so he could back into the spot. He knew immediately that he'd taken the wrong angle, so he put the car back in "Drive" and tried it again. This time, his effort was a little better but he was still a ways off. He put the car back in "Drive."

A month passed.

With trembling hands, Paul once again cranked the

steering wheel. He felt the back tire hit the curb. Another bad angle. He pulled forward.

"I hate to complain," said Doug, "but this is really taking a long time. Like, I think it's been about a month."

"Agreed," said Steve, with a head nod. "I know you're trying your best, Paul, but the game's been over for days now. Weeks, even. Also, I've never seen such a large pile of human feces inside a car before."

Paul stopped the car and took a deep breath.

"Guys, I'm trying my best," he said.

"We know you are, Paul," said Doug. "It's just that—and I think I mentioned this a couple weeks ago—I'm really quite hungry. We've already eaten through the center armrest and most of the passenger seat. But it's really not all that satisfying. I can actually see a pizza place on the next block. The moment we park, I'm heading there for sure. I'm so hungry at this point, I could eat two slices."

Steve rubbed his belly in agreement as he finished urinating on Doug's foot.

Paul reached into his beard and pulled out remnants of his leather wallet he'd tried eating a week earlier.

"Alright, fellas," said Paul. "Let's put all our positive energy together right now. I know we can do this if we stop focusing on the negative. I absolutely know it. Wait. We just ran out of gas."

Paul's friends were disappointed.

FIRST DATE

*H*i. I just wanted to call and tell you I'm looking forward to our date tonight.

Gretchen has told me a lot about you.

You'll recognize me at the restaurant because I'll be the one with the red rose on the table.

Also, I'll be wearing a brown sport coat.

In the event that there's another guy at the restaurant tonight wearing a brown sport coat with a red rose, there will be one more way to identify me.

I'll have a large plastic cone around my neck.

I know, I know. I was shocked at first as well. These kinds of cones are usually reserved for dogs.

It was my doctor's idea. I've had a couple moles removed in the past to be biopsied and I couldn't help but fiddle around with the stiches.

"Keep fiddling and we might have to go to drastic measures the next time you get a mole removed," Dr. Fong warned.

Well, here we are. Drastic measures.

It bothered me in the beginning. Truth be told, I almost drowned the first time I tried showering with it on. I simply wasn't expecting the cone to fill up with water so quickly.

And I've had to use scissors to cut out a plunging neckline on all my t-shirts so I can pull them over my cone.

Also, wiping my nether regions isn't easy when you can't see what or where you're wiping.

I gotta hand it to Dr. Fong, though. It's working. I haven't ripped into any stitches yet. So, it's not all negatives.

Well, that's the story about the dog cone around my neck.

I'm glad we got that out of the way.

See you later, elephant in the room.

Anyway, I'm excited about this restaurant we're going to tonight. It's a seafood tapas place with a halibut ceviche that I heard we definitely have to try. Their website shows an amazing cocktail list as well.

Who am I kidding?

I gotta assume there's a less than 10% chance you're still listening to this message.

Let's make it less than 3%.

It's because of the dog cone, isn't it?

ICE BREAKERS

*I*f this subway train happens to break down, these will probably be the conversation starters I'll use on those around me to help pass the time.

The Woman to My Left: Asian, mid-fifties, smug look on her face. She's holding a non-descript, brown purse. I could always ask if the purse happens to be new and where she might've purchased it from. If that doesn't work, I could say, "So, are you a gum or a mints kind of gal?" But, honestly, I can already see that her and I have nothing in common and the idea of talking to her for more than 30 seconds sounds excruciating.

The Man to My Right: Caucasian, late thirties, suit, tie and briefcase. He's a businessman. A man who does business. Once again, I'd have no idea where to start. I'd try to use business slang like "dividend" and "conference room". I could ask, "So, did the market seem bullish today?" If he said no, I'd ask him if it's the opposite of a bullish market, but I can't remember what that term is for the life of me. It's another animal. Badger? Is it a badger market? I don't know. Like the Asian woman with the purse, talking to the businessman would be a waste of our time.

The Man Currently Hiding Underneath My Seat: Clown

mask, holding knife, blood on clown outfit, medium build. NOW we're talking. Literally. See, this is the kind of person I WANT to get to know. This guy has a story to tell and I'd love to hear it. Where would I even start? I might ask him if he gets paid per party, or if it's hourly. I'd probably find out how his real shoes don't fall out of the oversized clown shoes when he walks. And I'd eventually get around to asking him whose blood is on his clown suit and if he plans to kill any or all of us. I hope the answer to the final question is no, but that's the fun of meeting new people. You can never really guess who they are until you get to know them!

PREGNANT

*M*eg took a final slurp of her tomato soup, set the spoon down and looked across the table at her husband, Mark.

"Mark, I feel like I need to explain something," said Meg.

Mark took a bite of his grilled cheese sandwich.

"What is it, honey?"

Meg leaned forward.

"These last couple months, you've been so amazing about talking to my little growing bump."

She lovingly rubbed her stomach. Mark laughed knowingly and smiled.

She continued.

"I can't believe how loving and caring you've been to what's growing inside. We've spent so many nights talking to my belly, telling it about us, listening, kissing my belly and even playing music for it! That's been incredible! One night, it's Miles Davis. The next night, it's Simon & Garfunkel. What you've been doing is really beyond belief."

Mark looked down and smiled.

"Well, it'll be worth it," he said.

Meg fiddled with her spoon a little and wiped her face with her napkin.

"So, the thing I need to explain to you..." she said slowly, "is that I'm not pregnant."

Mark looked up.

"You aren't?"

"No," she said. "I've just gotten kind of fat."

She paused to let it sink in a little.

"I've been hitting up Applebee's a ton recently."

Mark quietly looked down at the table.

"Are you being serious?"

"Yes," she said.

"So, I've been playing Beethoven for a stomach full of jalapeno poppers?"

Meg hesitated, and then nodded.

"I suppose."

Mark picked at a cuticle on his fingernail.

"So, you're sure you're not pregnant?" he asked.

"Yeah," she said. "I actually had my uterus removed about seven years ago."

"Oh."

Meg fiddled with a string on her sweatshirt.

"I was going to tell you sooner about this whole thing."

"Yeah," Mark said.

"I've been meaning to," said Meg.

Mark nodded.

"I probably should've done that a little sooner," she said.

Mark nodded again.

"I'm just not good about initiating those kinds of things," she said.

Mark knowingly shrugged.

"My bad," she said.

PILLOW TALK

"*H*ey, Bryan. It's me, your pillow. I'm smelling your head right now because it's on top of me. I might be wrong, but it seems like you're using Pert Plus 2-in-1 again. Tropical scent."

"Hey, Bryan. It's me, your pillow. When you leave for the day, your cat sleeps on top of me. I'm not trying to tattle right now—simply passing on some information. Also, your cat sucks."

"Hey, Bryan. It's me, your pillow. I've attempted to smother you a total of twenty-seven times now in hopes that you'd die. Don't take it personally. I was just having a bad day. Or 'days', plural."

"Hey, Bryan. It's me, your pillow. Sometimes when you sleep you say, 'I want to become a princess, mommy. I do, I do, I do, I do want to become a princess so bad. Oh, mommy, make me a princess right now. Do an abracadabra and make me a princess at this very moment.' Because I'm a pillow, I don't know what any of this means."

"Hey, Bryan. It's me, your pillow. I wish you wore more clothes when you slept. If I had legs, I'd leave the room. Instead, I'm stuck looking at your third nipple all night. You might have a fourth one as well. I can't tell if it's a scar or a nipple."

"Hey, Bryan. It's me, your pillow. I'm sure most guys your age cry themselves to sleep as often as you do. I don't have the stats in front of me right now, so I'm giving you the benefit of the doubt on this one."

"Hey, Bryan. It's me, your pillow. That spray bronzer you're using these days is killing me. Literally. I once was a new, white pillow. Now I look like a plate of pureed carrots."

"Hey, Bryan. It's me, your pillow. Sometimes the dog uses me as a humpy toy. It feels nice to be desired, but it's still kind of gross."

"Hey, Bryan. It's me, your pillow. I decided it is indeed a nipple. Lucky number four."

TOUGH QUESTIONS FROM KIDS

- Where do babies come from?
- Where do pets go when they die?
- I was just downstairs in Dad's trophy room. There are a lot of animals stuffed down there: a quail, a bear, two antelope, a few elk and a beaver. I get it —Dad likes to hunt. He took them to a taxidermist so that he can remember these prized kills. The only one I don't understand is why Grandpa was stuffed. Not only that, but why is he in a Speedo, wearing a Mexican wrestling mask and holding a harpoon? Kind of creepy, right?
- Where did we all come from?
- Why do some people do bad things?

ANTARCTICA, A POEM

*T*he ice calls me.
      Leave your comfort.
Your ideals.
Your home.
Awake from your slumber.
Step outside and go.
So I obey.
I'm lifted and I look down below.
And say goodbye.
To where I've been.
To what I know.
To my old life.
The journey gives me time to consider.
Curiosity swallows me whole.
What will this land of ice have for me?
What creatures will I see?
Hours pass.
The tip of the plane tilts down.
I know my adventure is close.
My mind wanders to another question.
Why didn't I bring a jacket?
Seriously, what was I thinking?

I'm not even sure I packed long sleeves.
Tank tops and Frisbees? Got those covered.
Three years of living on a frozen continent.
I knew I should've created an Items To Bring checklist.
Might get a little chilly.
Dang.

POST-BIRTH

*M*edically speaking, when a baby leaves the womb, one of the nurses is typically in charge of wiping off the afterbirth. But when Ronan Gibbons was born, that nurse had to take a phone call because her car was in the shop. Now 35, Ronan, unaware it's okay to take a shower to wash it off, remains covered in his afterbirth.

Below are some documented conversations that have taken place in recent years. Please be forewarned—they can be very difficult to read.

POTENTIAL EMPLOYER: I looked at your resume, Ronan. And I feel like everything checks out okay. There's just one thing.
RONAN: Was it my subpar performance at Hive Tech?
POTENTIAL EMPLOYER: No. It's that you're covered in afterbirth.

GIRL ON A DATE: Ronan, it seems like you're having trouble gripping the chopsticks.

RONAN: Yeah, I've never been good at this sort of thing. I'm a little bit of a klutz.

GIRL ON A DATE: Do you think that it also has something to do with the fact that your hands are soaked in a slippery layer of afterbirth?

RONAN: No.

COWORKER ON MONDAY MORNING: Hey, Ro-Ro. What'd you do this weekend?

RONAN: I went hiking.

COWORKER ON MONDAY MORNING: Oh, I thought you went on one of those kid's game shows where they pour slime on everyone.

RONAN: No. I just went for a hike.

CAR SALESMAN: I saw you checking out this car. She's a beauty. Selling it for $28,000.

RONAN: Can I take it for a test drive?

CAR SALESMAN: Sure, just give me a sec to put down the seat coverings reserved for middle-aged people still covered in afterbirth.

DONUT MAKER: Oh my gosh. I'm so sorry.

RONAN: For what?

DONUT MAKER: Did I accidentally spray you with the glaze machine?

RONAN: No. This is just afterbirth. I'm covered in afterbirth.

HANG IN THERE

*W*hatever happened to Cottonballs, that cute, little kitten hanging from the tree branch in the famous "Hang In There" poster?

Well, Cottonballs hung in there.

He hung in there, big time.

And then he fell. After a good seven minutes, his cute little baby kitten claws were unable to hold on to that branch for any longer and down he went.

For the most part, the fall was forgiving. Long, lush grass cushioned his tiny furry body. However, a rogue tree root tweaked his left hind leg, giving Cottonballs a noticeable limp.

Shaking off the pain, the kitten walked across the back lawn in the direction of his cat door. His owners, Pam and Edgar Walker of Oak Brook, Illinois, treated him well, giving him a gravy-soaked Friskies meal more frequently than he probably deserved. When Cottonballs reached his feeding dish, he lapped up his meal with great gusto.

Full and satisfied, Cottonballs found his favorite spot on the sun-drenched front porch and took a nap that lasted for five hours. If you'd been there, it would've melted your heart. Warm, cuddly and safe, Cottonballs slept peacefully.

The peace wouldn't last.

Over time, Cottonballs became ornery. Hostile. Reckless. Those who knew him best said he cracked from the tremendous pressure of being the face of "hanging in there". Even for a strong, growing cat, the weight was too heavy for his shoulders.

"What if I don't want to hang in there?" Cottonballs once snapped at Pawsome, a Main Coon from three houses down. "Everybody expects me to hang in there. All because of that stupid poster. But maybe I'm tired of hanging in there. You know? Maybe the very last thing I want to do in all the world is hang in there. Has anyone ever thought of that? Has anyone ever given one damn what ole Cottonballs thinks?"

By the time he finished his long-winded rant, Pawsome had wandered 15 feet away, more focused on licking the inside of his hind leg than listening to his friend's cry for help.

But the message was clear: Cottonballs was losing it.

By the age of 7, Cottonballs wore a mini-leather jacket most days and was stoned out of his mind on Mexican catnip. He'd only wander into his owner's house to vomit on Edgar's pillow. Out of boredom, he'd spray urine directly into the face of Thunder, the family Pomeranian. At one point, Cottonballs rolled a honey ham—the Walkers' dinner that night—through his litter box. The incident kept an anxiety-ridden Pam in bed for two days.

In 1994, Cottonballs ended up hopping in the back of a truck headed for Atlantic City. He'd spend his remaining days wandering up and down the boardwalk, disoriented, high and belligerent.

One of his last known conversations was with a seagull that lived near Harrah's Resort.

"I didn't ask for this," Cottonballs muttered. "I saw a tree branch. And I hung from it. And I tried to hang in there. I tried like crazy to hang in there. But at some point, you just have to let go."

Cottonballs paused and, for a brief moment, reflected on his life.

He then coughed up a hairball that included a worn-out $1 chip from Bally's and limped in the direction of the beach.

HOW TO LUGE

To prepare yourself for the luge, your primary objective needs to be getting yourself into the riding position.

This position involves lying on your back.

To achieve this position, start by doing the following:

1. Lie on your back

At this point, it's simply a matter of doing some double-checking to make sure you've positioned yourself correctly. Ask yourself, "Am I on my back?" If so, you're in the right position. If, say, you happen to be on your front side lying face down, you'd be in the wrong position. To be in proper luging position, you would have to roll over. By doing this, you'll be able to lie on your back. And lying on your back, as we stated earlier, is how you luge.

Once you've figured out how to lie on your back, all you need to do is put on a helmet and a skin-tight suit.

Happy luging.

NAVAL WARFARE

*T*raditional history books have no record of it. Even World War II historians have little knowledge of the event. And, yet, sooner or later everyone will hear about *The Story of When Glenn Almost Changed the Course of WW2 History by Attempting to Attack the Japanese on His Jet Ski.*

It was October of 1944 and the second World War had been going on for five years. On the water, tensions were coming to a head between the USA and Japan, culminating in the Battle of Leyte Gulf, possibly the largest naval battle in history.

Two weeks before that epic battle happened, Glenn Kramer got fired from his job at Sears Roebuck. He had worked in the appliance department in the Pomona, California store. Glenn was fired for keeping a large quantity of cold cut lunch meats in a refrigerator on the show room floor. His manager finally "put the two and two together" when he saw Glenn reclined on one of the couches eating his fifth sandwich of the day. There were mustard stains everywhere.

Distraught and depressed, Glenn decided to go on a month-long vacation in the Philippines. He ended up finding a cheap hut on one of the beaches in Maasin City.

Most of his days were spent drinking cheap vodka and

smoking the local herb. He would routinely pass out on the beach by noon, naked and sunburned.

From his location, he was certainly aware of all the naval activity nearby. The sights and sounds were nearly impossible to avoid. But World War II wasn't enough to distract Glenn from his sorrows of getting fired at Sears Roebuck.

That is, until the morning of October 25th.

Glenn woke up in his hut with a particularly bad hangover and a number of fresh bug bites. Sand fleas, most likely. That's when Glenn stumbled out of bed and propped himself up in the doorway.

"Man," Glenn said aloud, "those Japanese drive me batty! I just want to get some sleep!"

He calmly left his hut and walked in the direction of a bamboo pile nearby. A local village boy had told him the game-changing news that there was an early Kawasaki jet ski prototype hidden underneath and he had to check it out.

Without hesitation, Glenn dragged the jet ski to the water, revved it up and took off.

He started by doing a few loop-de-loops in the bay, constantly watching the shoreline to see if any chicks were checking him out. They weren't.

Glenn then got some decent air off a couple waves. Again, he checked the shoreline for chicks. Again, nothing.

Hearing heavy artillery fire around the bend in the Leyte Gulf, Glenn simply said, "It's time to end this now and forever."

Wearing only a tank top and a pair of corduroy shorts, Glenn revved the engine to the max and sped off toward the action.

As he turned the corner and saw the event taking place before his eyes, Glenn nearly fell off the jet ski. But he kept his composure and looked around for Enemy #1.

Far off across the water, he saw the Japanese cruiser named *Tama*. He knew if the USA were to win this battle, *Tama* needed to go down. So he set his sights and angled the nose of the jet ski directly at *Tama*.

As Glenn sped across the water amidst kamikaze airstrikes and heavy torpedo activity, he considered a lot of things. He thought about his country. He thought of his parents. He thought about eating sandwiches on the display couches at Sears Roebuck.

50 meters from his target, Glenn finally cleared his mind of all things. His one mission was to sink the *Tama* and help end the war.

About 30 meters from the target, Glenn let out a barbaric scream.

About 15 meters from the target, Glenn's jet ski started sputtering because it was almost out of gas.

By the time Glenn reached the bow of the ship, the jet ski was completely out of gas. The nose of the jet ski barely touched *Tama*.

From high above him on the ship, he heard a voice.

"Ya, baka," the Japanese soldier yelled. "Nani ga arimasu ka?"

(Translation: "Hey idiot. What gives?")

Glenn could only shrug and started dog paddling the jet ski away from the ship. When he got about 20 meters away, a thrown helmet nailed him in the head. It was from the Japanese soldier who was still quite upset and, evidently, had tremendous throwing accuracy.

Exhausted, Glenn finally reached the beach.

He went back to his hut where he drank vodka and smoked herb, naked.

The next day he got word *Tama* was torpedoed by an American submarine and sank, thus ending the Battle of Leyte Gulf.

Glenn leaned back, took a drag, and said, "You're welcome, America. You're frickin' welcome."

CHILDHOOD DREAMS

*W*ith a gentle touch, John tucked his 7-year-old child, Danny, in bed. As he reached over to turn off the light, Danny stirred.

"Papa?" asked Danny.

"Yes, Son?" replied his father.

"I've decided what I'm going to be when I get older," said Danny, with a sparkle in his eyes. "I'm going to be a racecar driver."

John took a deep breath and looked down at the floor.

"But you don't have any arms," he said.

Danny sat up in bed.

"But what if they could fix that, Papa?" said Danny. "What if scientists could design arms for me? You know, robot arms like C3PO! I'd be the talk of the town! Or what if they could make my steering voice activated? So that when I say 'left', the car turns left, and when I say 'right' it turns right. Don't you think they can do that, Papa? Don't you think I can become a racecar driver?"

His father thought about it.

"But you don't have any legs, either," he whispered.

Epilogue: Thanks to the efforts of many—his family, fundraisers, engineers—little Danny was able to fulfill his dream years later of becoming a racecar driver. A really, really, really crappy racecar driver.

COMPUTER PASSWORD

*P*assword entry: NYMets1986
> *Password incorrect. Please re-enter password.*
Password entry: JohnsonClan
> *Password incorrect. Please answer security question: What was the name of your first pet?*
Password entry: Wait. Which pet?
> *Answer incorrect. Please re-enter answer to security question.*
Password entry: But I had, like, three pets.
> *Answer incorrect. Please re-enter answer to security question.*
Password entry: Are you talking about my goldfish? Because his name was Gaylord.
> *Answer incorrect. Please re-enter answer to security question.*
Password entry: It's not Gaylord? Because my other pet, a dog, was named Gaylord as well.
> *Answer incorrect. Please re-enter answer to security question.*
Password entry: I also had a bird. But do birds really count as pets? Just because we put something in a cage with a place to crap doesn't mean it's a pet.

> *Answer incorrect. Please re-enter answer to security question.*

Password entry: I once had a hamster. I'd built an elaborate habitrail for him in the garage. He was fat and got stuck in one of the smaller tubes. Fearing I'd kill him if I pushed him out, I ended up taking that part of the tube out and poked some holes in the bottom for his feet to stick out so he could still walk around.

> *Answer incorrect. Please re-enter answer to security question.*

Password entry: He only lived four more days.

> *Answer incorrect. Please re-enter answer to security question.*

Password entry: It wasn't the best living situation for him, it turned out.

> *Answer incorrect. Please re-enter answer to security question.*

Password entry: His name was Barry.

> *Answer incorrect. Please re-enter answer to security question.*

Password entry: Barry.

> *Answer to the security question accepted. A new password will be sent to your email address.*

EMPLOYEE EVALUATION

*R*eview for: Barry Lawson, Submarine Assistant
Review given by: Mark Tynes, Submarine
Captain

Areas of success:

- Likeable personality
- Works hard

Areas of improvement:

- Five hours into our most recent voyage from
  Connecticut to Egypt, Barry realized he forgot to
  load the food onto the submarine. This food was
  supposed to provide meals to the crew for the
  entire journey. To remedy the situation, Tom
  Walters remembers hearing Barry say, "I do have a

cereal variety pack in my bag and I'd be happy to share that. As an FYI, I've already eaten both the Rice Krispies and one of the Apple Jacks."

- We also learned early on that Barry suffers from Irritable Bowel Syndrome. His ongoing flatulence caused three members to become violently sick for approximately five days.
- Despite our cramped, enclosed space, Barry insisted on applying a large amount of Eternity for Men cologne to his body every morning.
- Trying to emulate Sean Connery's role in *The Hunt for Red October*, Barry wore a fake white beard most of the time. This beard often fell off his face and would randomly appear on crewmembers' pillows, the commander's chair and the toilet seat.
- On Day 8, Barry tried operating what he thought was the coffee maker and instead launched a torpedo in the general direction of Brazil.
- Before leaving the harbor, I told the crew, "Guys, see this giant latch here at the top of the submarine? Please don't open it." On Day 2, I woke up from a nap to see Barry trying to jimmy the latch open with the boot from the Monopoly board game. When I asked him what he was trying to do, he said, "I want to take pictures of seagulls."

Next steps:

- We'll probably fire Barry.

BASKETBALL GAME RECAP

SPOKANE, WA—Last night pitted two of the state's top high school basketball teams against one another in an early season showdown. Kennedy High School hosted King's High School in its historic gym that was built in 1935.

The Kennedy Eagles are coming off a season in which they finished third in State. Going into Friday, they held a 7-1 record. The King's Knights were eliminated in the first round of the State Tournament last season but were undefeated with a 9-0 record heading into Friday.

Things got off to a slow start for both teams after tip-off. Marcus Thompson, all-league last season for the Knights, was held scoreless and the Eagle's exciting freshman point guard, Tim Flynn, had no assists. The score was 0-0 at the end of the quarter.

There was much of the same in the second quarter. No one scored a point. Paul Williams of Kennedy led all players with four rebounds.

No scoring in the third quarter either.

Same with the fourth.

Jimmy Anderson of King's finally managed to tip in the game winner in overtime, giving the Knights an exciting 2-0 victory.

It should be noted that Terrance Littlefield, the equipment manager for Kennedy, left the team's air pump in his friend Gerald's garage the night before. Which meant the entire game was played with an extremely flat basketball that dribbled no better than a day-old baguette.

When asked about the game afterward, Kennedy's Coach Dickson said, "Our zone defense looked horrible tonight. But if I'm honest, I'd say that playing with a completely deflated basketball hurt our game plan the most. I know this is just insider coach-talk, but basketballs are supposed to be round. Generally speaking. Like, picture a grape. Could be a green grape. Or red. Or purple. It might even be a yellow grape. But now picture that grape being a lot bigger. And it's not full of juice. It's full of air. Or at least it should be. That's the round shape I'm talking about. Anyway, I'm kind of a know-it-all when it comes to all-things basketball. In high school, I made varsity as a senior."

HONORARY ADDRESS

$\mathcal{A}$s the applause died down following Dean Thompson's beautiful commencement address, there was silence as an unknown student stepped up to the podium. The student nervously cleared his throat inches from the microphone.

"Faculty and students," he started, "my name is Jeff and I'm honored to give this address on our graduation day. Many of you don't know me or recognize me. There's a reason for that. Four years ago, on my first day of school as a freshman, I was stuffed into a locker because I was kind of a nerd. I've been there until I finally got out a few days ago. Thanks again, Janitor Evans. There was a bad lever on the locker, and it turns out you have to jiggle it a little bit to get it to open. I never thought to try that.

That said, I feel like my experience in that locker was invaluable. While I obviously didn't have the opportunity to get 'book smart', I learned so much about people just by watching and listening through the little slits in the metal. I learned that even the most popular kids in school have times when they just need to cry. I learned that, deep down, most kids our age are filled with large amounts of fear—about being accepted, about our futures, you name it. And I learned that no matter how much money our parents make or how fancy or crummy our houses are, we all simply want to be loved. I don't know many of you, mainly because I was stuffed in a locker for the last four years. But I hope as you move forward in life, you'll learn how to love others and, more than that, how to let yourself be loved. That's my greatest wish for all of us, the Class of 2013. Go Gators!"

Jeff stepped away from the podium to a very polite applause from all in attendance.

After the ceremony ended, Jeff was given an honorary degree.

He was then stuffed into a nearby locker by a few of the cool guys on the football team.

HOLIDAY FEAST

$\mathcal{W}$ith snow softly falling outside, the Timmerman family sat down to enjoy Christmas dinner. Mrs. Timmerman looked over at little Jane and, with a warm smile, asked her to put away her brand-new dolly, Miss Jasper. Jane obliged, hugging Miss Jasper tightly one more time before setting her below the Christmas tree.

"Lois, I've been waiting all day for your delicious Christmas ham," said Aunt Stacy.

"I think we ALL have, honey," said Mr. Timmerman.

Just then, little Pete looked over at the dog dish where Boxer, the family's Black Labrador, normally ate.

"Mommy," asked little Pete. "Why is there a pig eating out of Boxer's dish?"

Mrs. Timmerman froze. She could barely breathe as the realization hit her.

"If the Christmas ham is eating out of Boxer's dish," she said, slowly. "Then that means I...just...cooked...Boxer."

The family shrieked in horror. Mr. Timmerman quickly removed the tinfoil from the main dish on the table to reveal it was indeed Boxer. In fact, the collar was still on the animal, clearly identifying him as their beloved pet.

Grandma Alice immediately vomited, and the children

cried. The rest of the table sat in stunned silence, unable to move an inch.

A few minutes passed as the family tried to calm down.

Finally, Mrs. Timmerman spoke.

"Well," she said. "At least we have a large bowl of stuffing to eat."

Little Jane screamed at the top of her lungs. She pointed to Grandpa's chair. Grandpa was gone and in his place was a large bowl of stuffing.

"You mean we have a large bowl of Grandpa to eat!" shouted a terrified little Pete.

The family cried and screamed and vomited.

It took a while before anyone was able to regain his or her composure.

"This is the worst Christmas ever," said Uncle Len.

The family nodded their heads in agreement.

"Actually," chimed in Mr. Timmerman, "Christmas 2008 was pretty bad. Remember, I got that sweatshirt that was a little baggy on me? What am I, an XL?"

The family laughed.

"You're right, Dad," said little Jane. "But this sure is a close Number 2!"

There was a feeling of holiday peace as Mrs. Timmerman began serving up platefuls of Boxer and Grandpa.

NEW JOB

*H*ow was my first day at work?
Let me just say this: those people were the biggest group of a-holes I've ever met in my entire life. And, for the record, I never, ever enjoy using blue language like 'a-holes'. These people had my blood boiling from the very beginning.

Before I left my apartment this morning, I asked myself a question: should or shouldn't I bring my cat, Meow Tse Tung to work with me today?

Honestly, I couldn't think of a reason not to.

It's a fact that the best places to work are the ones that allow employees to bring in their dogs. It's also a fact that dogs are far more inferior to cats. Putting those two and two together had me packing Meow Tse Tung's things with a flourish.

Because first impressions are of the utmost importance, I knew the preliminary meeting with my boss had to go well. Which is why I put a skinny tie and sport coat on Meow Tse Tung and shook out a number of kitty treats on Mr. Douglass' desk.

You know what Mr. Douglass asked me? You'd assume his question would be, "Is Meow Tse Tung dressed in her 'Crockett' or 'Tubbs' outfit right now?" It wasn't. Instead, he barked, "Do you mind getting your cat off my desk?" How rude is that?

Around lunchtime, we had an all-company meeting to announce that we'd just lost 30% of our business. Right around the time the CEO began talking about layoffs, Meow Tse Tung started coughing up a hairball. I couldn't help but blurt out, "Licky licky makes sicky sicky!" The funny saying wasn't well-received. In fact, I overheard a girl in the marketing department say, "I hope your cat dies."

I suppose the final straw—in THEIR eyes—was near the end of the day when Meow Tse Tung pooped on a number of computer keyboards throughout the office. It was hilarious. She was wearing the Nelson Mandela outfit I made for her. So many bright colors.

As I left for the day, Mr. Douglass said, "Don't ever come back here again." Obviously, he got cut off before he could say "... without bringing more great outfits for Meow Tse Tung to wear around the office."

They'll learn to love Meow Tse Tung. I know they will.

AUTUMN LEAVES

*P*hillip Dykstra, a substitute teacher in the Boston area, removed his jacket as he walked through the front door to his small brownstone.

While unlacing his boots, he noticed there were a couple leaves stuck to one of the heels. It was autumn in Boston, and fallen leaves littered the sidewalks and streets.

To prevent visitors from slipping and falling, Phillip went downstairs to his storage room and grabbed his leaf blower. He put back on his boots and jacket and tramped outside.

Phillip flipped the switch, the leaf blower roared to life and he began blowing the leaves off his entryway and walkway.

Since it was a pleasant afternoon, Phillip didn't stop when he got to the bottom of his front stairs. Instead, he continued down the sidewalk, blowing the large pile of leaves as he went. When he got to the corner at the end of the block, the pile of leaves in front of him was up to his waist and about six feet wide.

Phillip's leaf blower had plenty of juice left in the tank, so he blew the pile to the next block. And then the next. And the next. By the following morning, Phillip had crossed the Massachusetts state line with his pile of leaves that was now about five stories high and fifty yards long.

Days and evenings passed as Phillip continued blowing. After three weeks, Phillip and his leaves moved into Wyoming. After stopping to enjoy a lemonade and an energy bar, Phillip blew his leaves into an open field.

He then looked ahead and quickly stopped in his tracks.

On the opposite side of this massive field, another tsunami of leaves was blowing toward him. After squinting his eyes and studying the situation, he noticed there was another man his age with a leaf blower, propelling his massive pile of leaves toward Phillip. It was obvious the other unkempt man had crossed many state lines with his pile of leaves as well.

Phillip refocused and blew his leaves toward the middle of the field. The other man did the same. The two piles of leaves rushed toward each other like armies clashing in the middle of the battlefield.

When the two leaf piles hit each other head-on, they immediately skyrocketed into the air. With so many leaves, it was hard deciphering what exactly was happening. Phillip looked up and, when a little of the chaos had calmed, he realized the airborne leaves were forming beautiful shapes and symbols—as long as both he and the other man kept their leaf blowers pointed toward each other.

The first shape was of a sailboat. The next one, a pineapple. The next one, a silhouette of Olympic powerhouse Mary Lou Retton, mid-dismount. Following that, an image of Brian May from Queen. Shapes formed one after another, swirling into perfect arrangements.

When he realized what he was witnessing, Phillip fought off a tear and gave the other leaf blower a thumbs-up. The other man gave the same gesture in return.

After nearly an hour of performing this aerial display, Phillip's leaf blower finally crapped out. As did the other guy's.

With the leaves still hovering high in the air, Phillip and the other man both shrugged, turned their backs to each other and walked toward where they'd come.

Falling to earth like a yellow, orange and brown meteor

shower, the leaves crashed down to their final resting spot: Old Man Johnson's backyard.

Old Man Johnson had just finished taking a slurp of some reheated broccoli soup when he glanced out his back window.

Seeing the thirty-story-high pile of leaves sitting there, Old Man Johnson put his spoon down, lowered his head and said to his dog, "Damn."

As he got up to grab his rake from the garage, he remembered he'd loaned it three months ago to his hipster neighbors who'd moved to Portland a couple weeks prior and never returned it.

Old Man Johnson sat back down and again turned to his dog and said, "Damn."

HORSE RACE INTERVIEW

*J*UAN THE JOCKEY: I feel like we ran a smart race. The tendency in any horse race is to try to jump out and get an early lead. But in a 10-furlong, you have to pace yourself. Don't get caught up in the emotion. Just sit back, trust yourself, trust your horse and be ready for that exact moment in the race when you need to shift into high gear. I think Lightning Rod and I did a great job of that during this race. And it allowed us to finish on top.

LIGHTNING ROD THE HORSE: What'd I think of the race? I had an angry little fella whipping me for more than a mile. I can't see how that could be enjoyable under any circumstance. You know what I typically get when I win a race? An oat bag. You know what I get when I typically lose a race? An oat bag. There's got to be something more to life than this. I've thought about Hollywood. I've got a buddy who was an extra in *Dances with Wolves*. He got groomed every day, he didn't have to ever wear blinders and Kevin Costner pet him once on the nose. How is that not the life? Costner petting you on the nose? Meanwhile, I've got Juan whispering in my ear with his horrible cottage cheese breath that I better win this race or he'll castrate me. That's my motivation. Win, or lose my testicles. Great life.

WORK EMAIL

From: Jake DuBose <jake.dubose@techfiles.com>
To: All Company <techfiles@techfiles.com>
Date: March 3, 2013 6:47 P.M.

Attention, Suckers.

It appears my four-year run at Tech Files has come to an end. This decision was made after MUCH deliberation last night—moments after I realized I won FRICKIN' POWER-BALL!!!! That's right, ladies and germs! Big Daddy Dubose is $580 million richer!!!! Hell, yes!

After I got over my initial shock, I thought about my job and my career. And I asked myself some deep questions.

Questions like, if I quit my job at Tech Files, would I miss seeing that pissant Mark Waters in the hallway every day? Hmmmmm, let me think about that. I believe the answer is NO. How many fishing stories can one guy bore the entire company with? Oh, sockeye salmon were really jumping in the Yakima River last weekend? Say, that's great, Mark.

You mind getting out of the way so I can get to the hazelnut Coffeemate?

And would I miss the daily wisdom I received from my boss, Fred Gough? You talk about a guy who should've been out of the game two decades ago. I'm not saying Fred can't still be useful in life. A lot of guys his age make great ushers at Minor League ballparks. Checking tickets, handing out stickers to the kids … that's all you, Fred. All you.

And would I miss seeing all the hot chicks who work in our office every time I walk through the front door? That was a total JK, everyone. You know we have the most mediocre talent around. I'd say Angela Trout is our best-looking chick and what is she? A four? I'm guessing the stewardess on my first trip to Barbados will be twenty times as hot as Angela Trout.

As a final word, I know Fred and the team are counting on me t o complete the rest of the Devansky project before the big pitch Monday morning. Given the important nature of this assignment, there's no way I'd let $580 million get in the way of helping others out. Another JK! You're on your own! You all really suck!

Sincerely,

Mr. $580 Million

From: Jake DuBose <jake.dubose@techfiles.com>
     To: All Company <techfiles@techfiles.com>
     Date: March 3, 2013 9:06 P.M.

Dear Fellow Tech File Employees,
     Upon closer examination, it appears I misread a number or two on my Powerball ticket. The bad news is I didn't win $580 million. The good news is I still won $1,500. That should help

pay for the repairs from my recent fender bender. (That elderly woman quietly reading at the bus stop came out of nowhere. Am I right?) And the GREAT news is that I get to return to Tech Files, the company I've always held so close to my heart. Assuming you'll have me.

You'll have me, right?

Your friend,

Jake

BREAKING UP: WHAT SHE REALLY MEANS

*S*HE SAYS: I want to break up with you.
SHE MEANS: I want to break up with you because you're a male meter maid.

SHE SAYS: It's not you, it's me.
SHE MEANS: Seriously, there are a thousand other careers you could have. But you've decided that meter-maiding is your calling in life? Really?

SHE SAYS: I just need some time to get to know Me.
SHE MEANS: Can't you even get a desk job as a police officer or something? That way I could at least tell my friends my boyfriend is a cop.

SHE SAYS: You'll always mean a lot to me.
SHE MEANS: Do you know how tired I am of hearing your meter maid stories? Every single one consists of a ticket recipient yelling at you for 15 minutes and you fighting off tears as you waddle back to your little cart.

SHE SAYS: Maybe we're better off as friends.

SHE MEANS: Of course, there was that one story about that high-speed chase you were involved in. The one where that guy tore up his ticket and went running off and your little cart couldn't catch up with him. What was your plan if you had gotten him? Hit him with your stick that has the little piece of chalk on the end?

SHE SAYS: We had some really good times.

SHE MEANS: They don't even let you carry a gun. How can you wear what essentially looks like a police officer's uniform and not be allowed to pack heat? It's like getting dressed up like a chef and having someone tell you that you can't handle the food.

SHE SAYS: Let's stay in touch.

SHE MEANS: Seriously, a meter maid?

YELP REVIEW FOR RANDALL BROTHERS MOVING

 osted by Gus Woodward, 4:07 PM, 3/12

My experience with Randall Brothers Moving was very hit and miss. Two guys, Rico and Dylan, showed up early. We were supposed to begin at 8:30 and they arrived at 8:15. My wife and I both appreciated this since our house was packed to the ceilings with boxes. The sooner we could get the truck loaded, the better.

Julie, my wife, provided coffee and breakfast biscuits for everyone. Rico took one bite of the biscuit, threw it in my wife's face and said, "Do I look like the type of guy who wants a lukewarm biscuit? Do I? Well, do I?" I felt like that was a bit out of line and I told him so.

After the snack, the guys began loading up the truck. Because my leg is broken from an illegal slide tackle during an adult league soccer game and since my wife's arms aren't the same length, both of us were unable to help the movers. We were surprised by their cheerful attitudes. For 20 solid minutes, they moved boxes from our house to the truck.

Then something happened that caught us off guard.

Rico and Dylan removed the plastic sheet from the couch. Dylan sat down while Rico plugged the TV into the wall and turned it on. The Super Bowl had just started. When I asked what they thought they were doing, Rico threw another biscuit at my wife's face. This surprised me since I thought we'd finished off all the biscuits.

Julie and I stood near the teetering boxes behind the couch as the two movers watched the game. Over the course of the next six hours, about ten or twelve of their friends arrived with beer and food and lounged around watching the game.

The Patriots won.

When the game was over, Dylan and Rico packed a few more boxes into the truck. Dylan then rolled our lawn mower down the street into busy traffic and turned to us and said, "Que pasa, senoritas?" while making a lewd gesture.

They then grabbed the keys to our new Nissan Leaf and drove off. We never saw them again.

Final Rating: I'll give them 4 out of 10 stars. While the move itself didn't go as planned, they arrived early. And punctuality goes a long way with the missus and me.

PETTING ZOO INTERVIEWS

*S*HEEP: I don't like being petted.
ANOTHER SHEEP: Me neither.
GOAT: I have a child's finger in my stomach right now.
PIG: I have a child missing one finger in my stomach right now.
ANOTHER SHEEP: My fur smells like corn dog.
TIGER: I still can't believe no one's said anything about me being in here.
ANOTHER PIG: Is it a rule that every child has to have sticky hands that smell like something cherry flavored and a little bit of urine? Kids are gross. And I'm a pig.
ANOTHER SHEEP: You know what's fun? It's when they pull my fur. I'm being sarcastic.
RABBIT: This week alone, I've nabbed five wallets from purses while the moms weren't paying attention.
SHEEP: When I think about how another career option would be to live on a picturesque farm with rolling hills and sea views in Scotland, I realize how blessed I am. I too am being sarcastic.
ANOTHER GOAT: Cotton candy gives me the runs.
ZOOKEEPER: I sit in there all day and not one child will pet me on the head even once. I'm so lonely. So, so lonely.

CRAZY

*C*all me crazy, but I'm so enamored with you. Your smile, your laugh, your whisper—I need little else from life.

And, sure, call me crazy, but you're the last thing I think of when I go to bed and the first thing I think of when I wake up.

You're my sunrise and my sunset. You really are.

And, yes, call me crazy, but each time you leave my place I go around collecting every strand of hair that came off your head.

I'll leave this pile of hair on the kitchen counter next to the butter dish while I go to my closet.

From my closet, I'll pull out a sewing machine, a decent amount of your clothes which I've taken, a plastic bag labeled "Barbara's Hair," a coffee cup with your lipstick stain on it, an antique pickle jar containing your chewed-off fingernails and a mannequin in the shape of your body that's been drenched with Yearning, your favorite perfume.

I'll pour myself a glass of a medium-bodied pinot noir, play a rare Matchbox Twenty acoustic set on my Bose and use my hot glue gun to attach your hair to the life-sized mannequin version of you. If I'm feeling creative, I'll cut up your clothes and use the sewing machine to make a look-at-me outfit that's perfect for the season.

When the clock hits 6:30, I'll load my sniper rifle and crouch behind the park bench across the street from where you work, waiting to take out anyone I see you talking to.

So, go ahead, call me crazy.

Crazy in love with you.

BOOK READING

*M*ore than 120 people squeezed in between the bookshelves and tables of the popular local bookstore, Double Booked. There was an excitement in the air since Double Booked had never had an author as popular as Jessica Landow do a reading. Ten straight mystery novels of hers had made the New York Times Best Sellers list, and her latest book, *Lost in Darkness*, was rumored to be her best to date.

Unlike most readings, many of the attendees weren't able to read the book since the first copies hadn't been available until midnight, less than 18 hours ago. Still, the chance to hear Landow read from her book in person was too great of a chance to pass up.

Martha Simpson, the owner of Double Booked, gave a brief introduction.

"We're honored to have one of the all-time greats with us tonight, ladies and gentlemen," she said. "I'm still pinching myself that *the* Jessica Landow is here in my tiny little bookstore. Most of you haven't had the chance to read her latest book, but let me just say, it's a page-turner! Without further ado, Ms. Jessica Landow."

For a book reading, there was quite a loud applause. Landow smiled and took her place front and center. She nodded her head in gratitude and sat down in the guest of honor's chair.

"Thank you so much for the warm reception," Landow said. "It's a privilege to be here today with so many great fans of my work. I'll be reading an excerpt from *Lost in Darkness* and will then be happy to answer any questions you might have and sign copies of the book."

Landow put on her reading glasses and opened up her latest novel. Members of the audience smiled at one another as they leaned forward to hear Landow's words.

"I'll be reading from page 683. This is chapter 34," Landow said, before clearing her throat. "'The door to the chicken coop swung open. Standing there was Jed Hanson, the grocery clerk. The long mystery had finally been revealed: Jed Hanson was the killer. The End.'"

The room was silent. Landow closed the book and took off her reading glasses.

"So, any questions?"

A woman in the front row slowly raised her hand.

"I suppose my only question," she began tentatively, "is why you just revealed who the killer is in your book."

Landow smiled.

"Did I *really* just tell you who the killer is?" she asked.

The woman who'd asked the question looked around at the other confused audience members.

Landow continued.

"All I said was that Jed Hanson was the killer. That could mean anything."

"Like what?" asked the woman in the audience.

"Well," said Landow. "Maybe the killer was Tina Walters, the school custodian?"

The woman in the audience shook her head.

"But you just told us that Jed Hanson was the killer."

"You're right," said Landow. "That's my mistake."

There was a pause and then the audience stood up and cheered wildly for her.

Because she was Jessica Landow.

FAMILY DOG

It's been nearly 20 years since the passing of Ducky, the family dog, and yet Michael still finds himself thinking about his old best friend. In fact, just the other day, he chuckled aloud while pouring himself some coffee because another Ducky memory hit him. It was of the time Ducky chewed through the tent during a camping trip just so he could sleep next to his family. Yes, the result was a wet dog gleefully spreading muddy paw prints all over the sleeping bags and pillows. But when Ducky finally plopped down in the middle of the tent, they knew he'd made the right decision by coming in. Dog or not, he was family.

Of course, there are other days where a different memory will hit him. Those times, Michael's reminded of a particular day back when he was 9. His bus had dropped him off a little early and he'd known he would have about a 10-minute wait before his mom arrived home from work and let him in the house. It was a little bit chilly. Not cold. Just not overly hot. Probably about 68 degrees but with a somewhat cool autumn breeze pushing its way through the neighborhood. He had forgotten his windbreaker on the bus and now stood on the porch, arms folded. Knowing he might eventually get to the point where he was going to be kind of cold, he did the only thing he thought he could do: he went to the backyard, gutted Ducky like Han Solo gutted the tauntaun in order to save Luke Skywalker, and fit as much of himself as he could inside Ducky's body to maximize the heat. After two or three minutes, he got kind of sweaty and decided to go back and sit on the front porch. His mom arrived 5 minutes later.

Looking back, Michael still doesn't know if he made the correct decision that day. That dog had meant so much to the family for so long. Ducky was always there whenever anyone needed a nose nudge of encouragement or a tail wag of happiness. But, gosh, it was just so cold on that day, Michael really felt like he'd had no other choice. Well, it was kind of cold. Or it was maybe about to get cold. Possibly.

To put his mind at ease, if only Michael could've known then what we know now: Ducky was a hardcore racist.

PANDA

Three years ago, the zookeepers at the Shanghai Zoo discovered that Sugarplum, a Giant Panda, had the ability to type on an old-fashioned typewriter. The following is just one of the many stories Sugarplum created. A collection of these sold for $2.5 million at a Sotheby's auction a few months ago.

AFDJASDLFKAS JDLFKASD JFFASD JFALSDKFJ ASLDF JASDLK FSJDLFK AJLGAKSDJFOWAIEFJAWOIRGNAI AORINAFVNADKV ASDNVKA LDNVALSDV KASNF LBKADFBN A IRNWOINWAEOAIWENFOW;AIEF-NAOE IQPWOASJDLAS DVK ASKD ASDJVKAS LDVJKASL DVJSALDV KJASDLVK ASJDVLK ASJVLSD KFBJAROINEROBIE RNBIAR BANORI BNEOR BNAORI BANRO WIANWROV AIWNV AWOVAN IOVAOEVAI SDVAS KDVOQIEASLVNSDVLKANSIOVA NSLD;VK ASLDVNA SKDLV ANSDLVK ASKDL VAWIEFOWAIEFNAO;IWENAOWEIFJQIWE-FAWEIFAWJEIFAOEJ EFIAJWE FIAW;EOFJ OAWEIFJ EFI AIEF JAWOEIFJA WEIFAWEJOIAWEGJAW-IGAW;ROGAJWOGIAWRGJAOWRIG WGIJARG IAJBAKAS JVALSKFJ ASLDFKJASEJNWEFKJAN SGA

RGSD BD BGA GA ERHR TH SRGNAS GKNAROGA
WREIGNAROGIANRGO AIRG AORGN AOERIG
NAEROG NAROA RBOANR IFANROAIWNEFOAIE
NFOABN IEBORNEST IOAWRETIOAWEI RWET
ISOUG AIODB AVJOI DCANSOIDVN AOIVBNS
AFDJASDLFKAS JDLFKASD JFFASD JFALSDKFJ ASLDF
JASDLK FSJDLFK AJLGAKSDJFOWAIEFJAWOIRGNAI
AORINAFVNADKV ASDNVKA LDNVALSDV KASNF
LBKADFBN A IRNWOINWAEOAIWENFOW;AIEF-
NAOE IQPWOASJDLAS DVK ASKD ASDJVKAS
LDVJKASL DVJSALDV KJASDLVK ASJDVLK ASJVLSD
KFBJAROINEROBIE RNBIAR BANORI BNEOR
BNAORI BANRO WIANWROV AIWNV AWOVAN
IOVAOEVAI SDVAS KDVOQIEASLVNSDVLKANSIOVA
NSLD;VK ASLDVNA SKDLV ANSDLVK ASKDL
VAWIEFOWAIEFNAO;IWENAOWEIFJQIWE-
FAWEIFAWJEIFAOEJ EFIAJWE FIAW;EOFJ OAWEIFJ
EFI AIEF JAWOEIFJA WEIFAWEJOIAWEGJAW-
IGAW;ROGAJWOGIAWRGJAOWRIG WGIJARG
IAJBAKAS JVALSKFJ ASLDFKJASEJNWEFKJAN SGA
RGSD BD BGA GA ERHR TH SRGNAS GKNAROGA
WREIGNAROGIANRGO AIRG AORGN AOERIG
NAEROG NAROA RBOANR IFANROAIWNEFOAIE
NFOABN IEBORNEST IOAWRETIOAWEI RWET
ISOUG AIODB AVJOI DCANSOIDVN AOIVBNS
AFDJASDLFKAS JDLFKASD JFFASD JFALSDKFJ ASLDF
JASDLK FSJDLFK AJLGAKSDJFOWAIEFJAWOIRGNAI
AORINAFVNADKV ASDNVKA LDNVALSDV KASNF
LBKADFBN A IRNWOINWAEOAIWENFOW;AIEF-
NAOE IQPWOASJDLAS DVK ASKD ASDJVKAS
LDVJKASL DVJSALDV KJASDLVK ASJDVLK ASJVLSD
KFBJAROINEROBIE RNBIAR BANORI BNEOR
BNAORI BANRO WIANWROV AIWNV AWOVAN
IOVAOEVAI SDVAS KDVOQIEASLVNSDVLKANSIOVA
NSLD;VK ASLDVNA SKDLV ANSDLVK ASKDL
VAWIEFOWAIEFNAO;IWENAOWEIFJQIWE-

FAWEIFAWJEIFAOEJ EFIAJWE FIAW;EOFJ OAWEIFJ
EFI AIEF JAWOEIFJA WEIFAWEJOIAWEGJAW-
IGAW;ROGAJWOGIAWRGJAOWRIG WGIJARG
IAJBAKAS JVALSKFJ ASLDFKJASEJNWEFKJAN SGA
RGSD BD BGA GA ERHR TH SRGNAS GKNAROGA
WREIGNAROGIANRGO AIRG AORGN AOERIG
NAEROG NAROA RBOANR IFANROAIWNEFOAIE
NFOABN IEBORNEST IOAWRETIOAWEI RWET
ISOUG AIODB AVJOI DCANSOIDVN AOIVBNS
AFDJASDLFKAS JDLFKASD JFFASD JFALSDKFJ ASLDF
JASDLK FSJDLFK AJLGAKSDJFOWAIEFJAWOIRGNAI
AORINAFVNADKV ASDNVKA LDNVALSDV KASNF
LBKADFBN A IRNWOINWAEOAIWENFOW;AIEF-
NAOE IQPWOASJDLAS DVK ASKD ASDJVKAS
LDVJKASL DVJSALDV KJASDLVK ASJDVLK ASJVLSD
KFBJAROINEROBIE RNBIAR BANORI BNEOR
BNAORI BANRO WIANWROV AIWNV AWOVAN
IOVAOEVAI SDVAS KDVOQIEASLVNSDVLKANSIOVA
NSLD;VK ASLDVNA SKDLV ANSDLVK ASKDL
VAWIEFOWAIEFNAO;IWENAOWEIFJQIWE-
FAWEIFAWJEIFAOEJ EFIAJWE FIAW;EOFJ OAWEIFJ
EFI AIEF JAWOEIFJA WEIFAWEJOIAWEGJAW-
IGAW;ROGAJWOGIAWRGJAOWRIG WGIJARG
IAJBAKAS JVALSKFJ ASLDFKJASEJNWEFKJAN SGA
RGSD BD BGA GA ERHR TH SRGNAS GKNAROGA
WREIGNAROGIANRGO AIRG AORGN AOERIG
NAEROG NAROA RBOANR IFANROAIWNEFOAIE
NFOABN IEBORNEST IOAWRETIOAWEI RWET
ISOUG AIODB AVJOI DCANSOIDVN AOIVBNS
AFDJASDLFKAS JDLFKASD JFFASD JFALSDKFJ ASLDF
JASDLK FSJDLFK AJLGAKSDJFOWAIEFJAWOIRGNAI
AORINAFVNADKV ASDNVKA LDNVALSDV KASNF
LBKADFBN A IRNWOINWAEOAIWENFOW;AIEF-
NAOE IQPWOASJDLAS DVK ASKD ASDJVKAS
LDVJKASL DVJSALDV KJASDLVK ASJDVLK ASJVLSD
KFBJAROINEROBIE RNBIAR BANORI BNEOR

BNAORI BANRO WIANWROV AIWNV AWOVAN
IOVAOEVAI SDVAS KDVOQIEASLVNSDVLKANSIOVA
NSLD;VK ASLDVNA SKDLV ANSDLVK ASKDL
VAWIEFOWAIEFNAO;IWENAOWEIFJQIWE-
FAWEIFAWJEIFAOEJ EFIAJWE FIAW;EOFJ OAWEIFJ
EFI AIEF JAWOEIFJA WEIFAWEJOIAWEGJAW-
IGAW;ROGAJWOGIAWRGJAOWRIG WGIJARG
IAJBAKAS JVALSKFJ ASLDFKJASEJNWEFKJAN SGA
RGSD BD BGA GA ERHR TH SRGNAS GKNAROGA
WREIGNAROGIANRGO AIRG AORGN AOERIG
NAEROG NAROA RBOANR IFANROAIWNEFOAIE
NFOABN IEBORNEST IOAWRETIOAWEI RWET
ISOUG AIODB AVJOI DCANSOIDVN AOIVBNS
AFDJASDLFKAS JDLFKASD JFFASD JFALSDKFJ ASLDF
JASDLK FSJDLFK AJLGAKSDJFOWAIEFJAWOIRGNAI
AORINAFVNADKV ASDNVKA LDNVALSDV KASNF
LBKADFBN A IRNWOINWAEOAIWENFOW;AIEF-
NAOE IQPWOASJDLAS DVK ASKD ASDJVKAS
LDVJKASL DVJSALDV KJASDLVK ASJDVLK ASJVLSD
KFBJAROINEROBIE RNBIAR BANORI BNEOR
BNAORI BANRO WIANWROV AIWNV AWOVAN
IOVAOEVAI SDVAS KDVOQIEASLVNSDVLKANSIOVA
NSLD;VK ASLDVNA SKDLV ANSDLVK ASKDL
VAWIEFOWAIEFNAO;IWENAOWEIFJQIWE-
FAWEIFAWJEIFAOEJ EFIAJWE FIAW;EOFJ OAWEIFJ
EFI AIEF JAWOEIFJA WEIFAWEJOIAWEGJAW-
IGAW;ROGAJWOGIAWRGJAOWRIG WGIJARG
IAJBAKAS JVALSKFJ ASLDFKJASEJNWEFKJAN SGA
RGSD BD BGA GA ERHR TH SRGNAS GKNAROGA
WREIGNAROGIANRGO AIRG AORGN AOERIG
NAEROG NAROA RBOANR IFANROAIWNEFOAIE
NFOABN IEBORNEST IOAWRETIOAWEI RWET
ISOUG AIODB AVJOI DCANSOIDVN AOIVBNS
AFDJASDLFKAS JDLFKASD JFFASD JFALSDKFJ ASLDF
JASDLK FSJDLFK AJLGAKSDJFOWAIEFJAWOIRGNAI
AORINAFVNADKV ASDNVKA LDNVALSDV KASNF

LBKADFBN A IRNWOINWAEOAIWENFOW;AIEF-
NAOE IQPWOASJDLAS DVK ASKD ASDJVKAS
LDVJKASL DVJSALDV KJASDLVK ASJDVLK ASJVLSD
KFBJAROINEROBIE RNBIAR BANORI BNEOR
BNAORI BANRO WIANWROV AIWNV AWOVAN
IOVAOEVAI SDVAS KDVOQIEASLVNSDVLKANSIOVA
NSLD;VK ASLDVNA SKDLV ANSDLVK ASKDL
VAWIEFOWAIEFNAO;IWENAOWEIFJQIWE-
FAWEIFAWJEIFAOEJ EFIAJWE FIAW;EOFJ OAWEIFJ
EFI AIEF JAWOEIFJA WEIFAWEJOIAWEGJAW-
IGAW;ROGAJWOGIAWRGJAOWRIG WGIJARG
IAJBAKAS JVALSKFJ ASLDFKJASEJNWEFKJAN SGA
RGSD BD BGA GA ERHR TH SRGNAS GKNAROGA
WREIGNAROGIANRGO AIRG AORGN AOERIG
NAEROG NAROA RBOANR IFANROAIWNEFOAIE
NFOABN IEBORNEST IOAWRETIOAWEI RWET
ISOUG AIODB AVJOI DCANSOIDVN AOIVBNS
DFBOIAFDN O;IFB ANOSBFIAN SOIREN AERIOA
SE;FIAOS GNIAOSEFIN ASOIR; RIEAUADJFKASLJFAL-
SJEIEFAEBKANBKALSDK ADJFSKD JDK FJ DFSDKJ
FLWKE FJWEK FWJEK WLEJF KLWE FJK
JEFWIEORQUEIORUE W BKDNFVKDFNDKLFBNS-
DLKFNB KFKWENF WEKN WEFKWEFNALEKN-
FWEKLFNWELKFWNEKFNW EF
WKEFNWLEFKNWEKLFNWE FKWLE FKLW EFWK
ELKW EFKLWE KFLWE FKWNELKFNWELFK-
WNGLAKRGN KLNGERGNSJNSJKRNNKJASNFLQK-
WNQLKWEJQWLK QW J QWJQLKWJQLWK EQW
LQW JQLW KQLWJ QLKWJ LK JLKJLSKJSLDKBN-
BVLXNBLXKCBNLCKBNDLK WLEKFNWEKFWLNEK-
FLWENFKWLEFNKWELFNWKELFNWKELFNWLEKNF
EW FWEJRWIEOUFIOWEUGWOUPRUWEPOIU
EUIWEO EIUR REKNFKWALENF ELK HGHWEJGH-
WEOHWERH3R283R8F 238 238 238 FAWNGKASLD-
NVLVNASDKVNA;VWKNNWLE;VNAKVAKLNVLKV SL
WKENRL3RK42N34 3KR 23K 23KR 23KJ JVAKLV-

NADBKLNAKVBLANSDKFLA;SDNFKLSNFSKDF;
AFDJASDLFKAS JDLFKASD JFFASD JFALSDKFJ ASLDF
JASDLK FSJDLFK AJLGAKSDJFOWAIEFJAWOIRGNAI
AORINAFVNADKV ASDNVKA LDNVALSDV KASNF
LBKADFBN A IRNWOINWAEOAIWENFOW;AIEF-
NAOE IQPWOASJDLAS DVK ASKD ASDJVKAS
LDVJKASL DVJSALDV KJASDLVK ASJDVLK ASJVLSD
KFBJAROINEROBIE RNBIAR BANORI BNEOR
BNAORI BANRO WIANWROV AIWNV AWOVAN
IOVAOEVAI SDVAS KDVOQIEASLVNSDVLKANSIOVA
NSLD;VK ASLDVNA SKDLV ANSDLVK ASKDL
VAWIEFOWAIEFNAO;IWENAOWEIFJQIWE-
FAWEIFAWJEIFAOEJ EFIAJWE FIAW;EOFJ OAWEIFJ
EFI AIEF JAWOEIFJA WEIFAWEJOIAWEGJAW-
IGAW;ROGAJWOGIAWRGJAOWRIG WGIJARG
IAJBAKAS JVALSKFJ ASLDFKJASEJNWEFKJAN SGA
RGSD BD BGA GA ERHR TH SRGNAS GKNAROGA
WREIGNAROGIANRGO AIRG AORGN AOERIG
NAEROG NAROA RBOANR IFANROAIWNEFOAIE
NFOABN IEBORNEST IOAWRETIOAWEI RWET
ISOUG AIODB AVJOI DCANSOIDVN AOIVBNS
AFDJASDLFKAS JDLFKASD JFFASD JFALSDKFJ ASLDF
JASDLK FSJDLFK AJLGAKSDJFOWAIEFJAWOIRGNAI
AORINAFVNADKV ASDNVKA LDNVALSDV KASNF
LBKADFBN A IRNWOINWAEOAIWENFOW;AIEF-
NAOE IQPWOASJDLAS DVK ASKD ASDJVKAS
LDVJKASL DVJSALDV KJASDLVK ASJDVLK ASJVLSD
KFBJAROINEROBIE RNBIAR BANORI BNEOR
BNAORI BANRO WIANWROV AIWNV AWOVAN
IOVAOEVAI SDVAS KDVOQIEASLVNSDVLKANSIOVA
NSLD;VK ASLDVNA SKDLV ANSDLVK ASKDL
VAWIEFOWAIEFNAO;IWENAOWEIFJQIWE-
FAWEIFAWJEIFAOEJ EFIAJWE FIAW;EOFJ OAWEIFJ
EFI AIEF JAWOEIFJA WEIFAWEJOIAWEGJAW-
IGAW;ROGAJWOGIAWRGJAOWRIG WGIJARG
IAJBAKAS JVALSKFJ ASLDFKJASEJNWEFKJAN SGA

RGSD BD BGA GA ERHR TH SRGNAS GKNAROGA WREIGNAROGIANRGO AIRG AORGN AOERIG NAEROG NAROA RBOANR IFANROAIWNEFOAIE NFOABN IEBORNEST IOAWRETIOAWEI RWET ISOUG AIODB AVJOI DCANSOIDVN AOIVBNS AFDJASDLFKAS JDLFKASD JFFASD JFALSDKFJ ASLDF JASDLK FSJDLFK AJLGAKSDJFOWAIEFJAWOIRGNAI AORINAFVNADKV ASDNVKA LDNVALSDV KASNF LBKADFBN A IRNWOINWAEOAIWENFOW;AIEF-NAOE IQPWOASJDLAS DVK ASKD ASDJVKAS LDVJKASL DVJSALDV KJASDLVK ASJDVLK ASJVLSD KFBJAROINEROBIE RNBIAR BANORI BNEOR BNAORI BANRO WIANWROV AIWNV AWOVAN IOVAOEVAI SDVAS KDVOQIEASLVNSDVLKANSIOVA NSLD;VK ASLDVNA SKDLV ANSDLVK ASKDL VAWIEFOWAIEFNAO;IWENAOWEIFJQIWE-FAWEIFAWJEIFAOEJ EFIAJWE FIAW;EOFJ OAWEIFJ EFI AIEF JAWOEIFJA WEIFAWEJOIAWEGJAW-IGAW;ROGAJWOGIAWRGJAOWRIG WGIJARG IAJBAKAS JVALSKFJ ASLDFKJASEJNWEFKJAN SGA RGSD BD BGA GA ERHR TH SRGNAS GKNAROGA WREIGNAROGIANRGO AIRG AORGN AOERIG NAEROG NAROA RBOANR IFANROAIWNEFOAIE NFOABN IEBORNEST IOAWRETIOAWEI RWET ISOUG AIODB AVJOI DCANSOIDVN AOIVBNS AFDJASDLFKAS JDLFKASD JFFASD JFALSDKFJ ASLDF JASDLK FSJDLFK AJLGAKSDJFOWAIEFJAWOIRGNAI AORINAFVNADKV ASDNVKA LDNVALSDV KASNF LBKADFBN A IRNWOINWAEOAIWENFOW;AIEF-NAOE IQPWOASJDLAS DVK ASKD ASDJVKAS LDVJKASL DVJSALDV KJASDLVK ASJDVLK ASJVLSD KFBJAROINEROBIE RNBIAR BANORI BNEOR BNAORI BANRO WIANWROV AIWNV AWOVAN IOVAOEVAI SDVAS KDVOQIEASLVNSDVLKANSIOVA NSLD;VK ASLDVNA SKDLV ANSDLVK ASKDL VAWIEFOWAIEFNAO;IWENAOWEIFJQIWE-

FAWEIFAWJEIFAOEJ EFIAJWE FIAW;EOFJ OAWEIFJ
EFI AIEF JAWOEIFJA WEIFAWEJOIAWEGJAW-
IGAW;ROGAJWOGIAWRGJAOWRIG WGIJARG
IAJBAKAS JVALSKFJ ASLDFKJASEJNWEFKJAN SGA
RGSD BD BGA GA ERHR TH SRGNAS GKNAROGA
WREIGNAROGIANRGO AIRG AORGN AOERIG
NAEROG NAROA RBOANR IFANROAIWNEFOAIE
NFOABN IEBORNEST IOAWRETIOAWEI RWET
ISOUG AIODB AVJOI DCANSOIDVN AOIVBNS
AFDJASDLFKAS JDLFKASD JFFASD JFALSDKFJ ASLDF
JASDLK FSJDLFK AJLGAKSDJFOWAIEFJAWOIRGNAI
AORINAFVNADKV ASDNVKA LDNVALSDV KASNF
LBKADFBN A IRNWOINWAEOAIWENFOW;AIEF-
NAOE IQPWOASJDLAS DVK ASKD ASDJVKAS
LDVJKASL DVJSALDV KJASDLVK ASJDVLK ASJVLSD
KFBJAROINEROBIE RNBIAR BANORI BNEOR
BNAORI BANRO WIANWROV AIWNV AWOVAN
IOVAOEVAI SDVAS KDVOQIEASLVNSDVLKANSIOVA
NSLD;VK ASLDVNA SKDLV ANSDLVK ASKDL
VAWIEFOWAIEFNAO;IWENAOWEIFJQIWE-
FAWEIFAWJEIFAOEJ EFIAJWE FIAW;EOFJ OAWEIFJ
EFI AIEF JAWOEIFJA WEIFAWEJOIAWEGJAW-
IGAW;ROGAJWOGIAWRGJAOWRIG WGIJARG
IAJBAKAS JVALSKFJ ASLDFKJASEJNWEFKJAN SGA
RGSD BD BGA GA ERHR TH SRGNAS GKNAROGA
WREIGNAROGIANRGO AIRG AORGN AOERIG
NAEROG NAROA RBOANR IFANROAIWNEFOAIE
NFOABN IEBORNEST IOAWRETIOAWEI RWET
ISOUG AIODB AVJOI DCANSOIDVN AOIVBNS
AFDJASDLFKAS JDLFKASD JFFASD JFALSDKFJ ASLDF
JASDLK FSJDLFK AJLGAKSDJFOWAIEFJAWOIRGNAI
AORINAFVNADKV ASDNVKA LDNVALSDV KASNF
LBKADFBN A IRNWOINWAEOAIWENFOW;AIEF-
NAOE IQPWOASJDLAS DVK ASKD ASDJVKAS
LDVJKASL DVJSALDV KJASDLVK ASJDVLK ASJVLSD
KFBJAROINEROBIE RNBIAR BANORI BNEOR

BNAORI BANRO WIANWROV AIWNV AWOVAN IOVAOEVAI SDVAS KDVOQIEASLVNSDVLKANSIOVA NSLD;VK ASLDVNA SKDLV ANSDLVK ASKDL VAWIEFOWAIEFNAO;IWENAOWEIFJQIWE-FAWEIFAWJEIFAOEJ EFIAJWE FIAW;EOFJ OAWEIFJ EFI AIEF JAWOEIFJA WEIFAWEJOIAWEGJAW-IGAW;ROGAJWOGIAWRGJAOWRIG WGIJARG IAJBAKAS JVALSKFJ ASLDFKJASEJNWEFKJAN SGA RGSD BD BGA GA ERHR TH SRGNAS GKNAROGA WREIGNAROGIANRGO AIRG AORGN AOERIG NAEROG NAROA RBOANR IFANROAIWNEFOAIE NFOABN IEBORNEST IOAWRETIOAWEI RWET ISOUG AIODB AVJOI DCANSOIDVN AOIVBNS AFDJASDLFKAS JDLFKASD JFFASD JFALSDKFJ ASLDF JASDLK FSJDLFK AJLGAKSDJFOWAIEFJAWOIRGNAI AORINAFVNADKV ASDNVKA LDNVALSDV KASNF LBKADFBN A IRNWOINWAEOAIWENFOW;AIEF-NAOE IQPWOASJDLAS DVK ASKD ASDJVKAS LDVJKASL DVJSALDV KJASDLVK ASJDVLK ASJVLSD KFBJAROINEROBIE RNBIAR BANORI BNEOR BNAORI BANRO WIANWROV AIWNV AWOVAN IOVAOEVAI SDVAS KDVOQIEASLVNSDVLKANSIOVA NSLD;VK ASLDVNA SKDLV ANSDLVK ASKDL VAWIEFOWAIEFNAO;IWENAOWEIFJQIWE-FAWEIFAWJEIFAOEJ EFIAJWE FIAW;EOFJ OAWEIFJ EFI AIEF JAWOEIFJA WEIFAWEJOIAWEGJAW-IGAW;ROGAJWOGIAWRGJAOWRIG WGIJARG IAJBAKAS JVALSKFJ ASLDFKJASEJNWEFKJAN SGA RGSD BD BGA GA ERHR TH SRGNAS GKNAROGA WREIGNAROGIANRGO AIRG AORGN AOERIG NAEROG NAROA RBOANR IFANROAIWNEFOAIE NFOABN IEBORNEST IOAWRETIOAWEI RWET ISOUG AIODB AVJOI DCANSOIDVN AOIVBNS DFBOIAFDN O;IFB ANOSBFIAN SOIREN AERIOA SE;FIAOS GNIAOSEFIN ASOIR; RIEAUADJFKASLJFAL-SJEIEFAEBKANBKALSDK ADJFSKD JDK FJ DFSDKJ

FLWKE   FJWEK   FWJEK   WLEJF   KLWE   FJK
JEFWIEORQUEIORUE   W   BKDNFVKDFNDKLFBNS-
DLKFNB   KFKWENF   WEKN   WEFKWEFNALEKN-
FWEKLFNWELKFWNEKFNW   EF
WKEFNWLEFKNWEKLFNWE   FKWLE   FKLW   EFWK
ELKW   EFKLWE   KFLWE   FKWNELKFNWELFK-
WNGLAKRGN   KLNGERGNSJNSJKRNNKJASNFLQK-
WNQLKWEJQWLK   QW   J   QWJQLKWJQLWK   EQW
LQW   JQLW   KQLWJ   QLKWJ   LK   JLKJLSKJSLDKBN-
BVLXNBLXKCBNLCKBNDLK   WLEKFNWEKFWLNEK-
FLWENFKWLEFNKWELF   AFDJASDLFKAS   JDLFKASD
JFFASD JFALSDKFJ ASLDF JASDLK FSJDLFK AJLGAKS-
DJFOWAIEFJAWOIRGNAI   AORINAFVNADKV
ASDNVKA   LDNVALSDV   KASNF   LBKADFBN   A
IRNWOINWAEOAIWENFOW;AIEFNAOE
IQPWOASJDLAS   DVK   ASKD   ASDJVKAS   LDVJKASL
DVJSALDV   KJASDLVK   ASJDVLK   ASJVLSD
KFBJAROINEROBIE   RNBIAR   BANORI   BNEOR
BNAORI   BANRO   WIANWROV   AIWNV   AWOVAN
IOVAOEVAI   SDVAS   KDVOQIEASLVNSDVLKANSIOVA
NSLD;VK   ASLDVNA   SKDLV   ANSDLVK   ASKDL
VAWIEFOWAIEFNAO;IWENAOWEIFJQIWE-
FAWEIFAWJEIFAOEJ   EFIAJWE   FIAW;EOFJ   OAWEIFJ
EFI   AIEF   JAWOEIFJA   WEIFAWEJOIAWEGJAW-
IGAW;ROGAJWOGIAWRGJAOWRIG   WGIJARG
IAJBAKAS   JVALSKFJ   ASLDFKJASEJNWEFKJAN   SGA
RGSD   BD   BGA   GA   ERHR   TH   SRGNAS   GKNAROGA
WREIGNAROGIANRGO   AIRG   AORGN   AOERIG
NAEROG   NAROA   RBOANR   IFANROAIWNEFOAIE
NFOABN   IEBORNEST   IOAWRETIOAWEI   RWET
ISOUG   AIODB   AVJOI   DCANSOIDVN   AOIVBNS
AFDJASDLFKAS   JDLFKASD   JFFASD   JFALSDKFJ   ASLDF
JASDLK   FSJDLFK   AJLGAKSDJFOWAIEFJAWOIRGNAI
AORINAFVNADKV   ASDNVKA   LDNVALSDV   KASNF
LBKADFBN   A   IRNWOINWAEOAIWENFOW;AIEF-
NAOE   IQPWOASJDLAS   DVK   ASKD   ASDJVKAS

LDVJKASL DVJSALDV KJASDLVK ASJDVLK ASJVLSD KFBJAROINEROBIE RNBIAR BANORI BNEOR BNAORI BANRO WIANWROV AIWNV AWOVAN IOVAOEVAI SDVAS KDVOQIEASLVNSDVLKANSIOVA NSLD;VK ASLDVNA SKDLV ANSDLVK ASKDL VAWIEFOWAIEFNAO;IWENAOWEIFJQIWE-FAWEIFAWJEIFAOEJ EFIAJWE FIAW;EOFJ OAWEIFJ EFI AIEF JAWOEIFJA WEIFAWEJOIAWEGJAW-IGAW;ROGAJWOGIAWRGJAOWRIG WGIJARG IAJBAKAS JVALSKFJ ASLDFKJASEJNWEFKJAN SGA RGSD BD BGA GA ERHR TH SRGNAS GKNAROGA WREIGNAROGIANRGO AIRG AORGN AOERIG NAEROG NAROA RBOANR IFANROAIWNEFOAIE NFOABN IEBORNEST IOAWRETIOAWEI RWET ISOUG AIODB AVJOI DCANSOIDVN AOIVBNS AFDJASDLFKAS JDLFKASD JFFASD JFALSDKFJ ASLDF JASDLK FSJDLFK AJLGAKSDJFOWAIEFJAWOIRGNAI AORINAFVNADKV ASDNVKA LDNVALSDV KASNF LBKADFBN A IRNWOINWAEOAIWENFOW;AIEF-NAOE IQPWOASJDLAS DVK ASKD ASDJVKAS LDVJKASL DVJSALDV KJASDLVK ASJDVLK ASJVLSD KFBJAROINEROBIE RNBIAR BANORI BNEOR BNAORI BANRO WIANWROV AIWNV AWOVAN IOVAOEVAI SDVAS KDVOQIEASLVNSDVLKANSIOVA NSLD;VK ASLDVNA SKDLV ANSDLVK ASKDL VAWIEFOWAIEFNAO;IWENAOWEIFJQIWE-FAWEIFAWJEIFAOEJ EFIAJWE FIAW;EOFJ OAWEIFJ EFI AIEF JAWOEIFJA WEIFAWEJOIAWEGJAW-IGAW;ROGAJWOGIAWRGJAOWRIG WGIJARG IAJBAKAS JVALSKFJ ASLDFKJASEJNWEFKJAN SGA RGSD BD BGA GA ERHR TH SRGNAS GKNAROGA WREIGNAROGIANRGO AIRG AORGN AOERIG NAEROG NAROA RBOANR IFANROAIWNEFOAIE NFOABN IEBORNEST IOAWRETIOAWEI RWET ISOUG AIODB AVJOI DCANSOIDVN AOIVBNS AFDJASDLFKAS JDLFKASD JFFASD JFALSDKFJ ASLDF

JASDLK FSJDLFK AJLGAKSDJFOWAIEFJAWOIRGNAI
AORINAFVNADKV ASDNVKA LDNVALSDV KASNF
LBKADFBN A IRNWOINWAEOAIWENFOW;AIEF-
NAOE IQPWOASJDLAS DVK ASKD ASDJVKAS
LDVJKASL DVJSALDV KJASDLVK ASJDVLK ASJVLSD
KFBJAROINEROBIE RNBIAR BANORI BNEOR
BNAORI BANRO WIANWROV AIWNV AWOVAN
IOVAOEVAI SDVAS KDVOQIEASLVNSDVLKANSIOVA
NSLD;VK ASLDVNA SKDLV ANSDLVK ASKDL
VAWIEFOWAIEFNAO;IWENAOWEIFJQIWE-
FAWEIFAWJEIFAOEJ EFIAJWE FIAW;EOFJ OAWEIFJ
EFI AIEF JAWOEIFJA WEIFAWEJOIAWEGJAW-
IGAW;ROGAJWOGIAWRGJAOWRIG WGIJARG
IAJBAKAS JVALSKFJ ASLDFKJASEJNWEFKJAN SGA
RGSD BD BGA GA ERHR TH SRGNAS GKNAROGA
WREIGNAROGIANRGO AIRG AORGN AOERIG
NAEROG NAROA RBOANR IFANROAIWNEFOAIE
NFOABN IEBORNEST IOAWRETIOAWEI RWET
ISOUG AIODB AVJOI DCANSOIDVN AOIVBNS
AFDJASDLFKAS JDLFKASD JFFASD JFALSDKFJ ASLDF
JASDLK FSJDLFK AJLGAKSDJFOWAIEFJAWOIRGNAI
AORINAFVNADKV ASDNVKA LDNVALSDV KASNF
LBKADFBN A IRNWOINWAEOAIWENFOW;AIEF-
NAOE IQPWOASJDLAS DVK ASKD ASDJVKAS
LDVJKASL DVJSALDV KJASDLVK ASJDVLK ASJVLSD
KFBJAROINEROBIE RNBIAR BANORI BNEOR
BNAORI BANRO WIANWROV AIWNV AWOVAN
IOVAOEVAI SDVAS KDVOQIEASLVNSDVLKANSIOVA
NSLD;VK ASLDVNA SKDLV ANSDLVK ASKDL
VAWIEFOWAIEFNAO;IWENAOWEIFJQIWE-
FAWEIFAWJEIFAOEJ EFIAJWE FIAW;EOFJ OAWEIFJ
EFI AIEF JAWOEIFJA WEIFAWEJOIAWEGJAW-
IGAW;ROGAJWOGIAWRGJAOWRIG WGIJARG
IAJBAKAS JVALSKFJ ASLDFKJASEJNWEFKJAN SGA
RGSD BD BGA GA ERHR TH SRGNAS GKNAROGA
WREIGNAROGIANRGO AIRG AORGN AOERIG

NAEROG NAROA RBOANR IFANROAIWNEFOAIE
NFOABN IEBORNEST IOAWRETIOAWEI RWET
ISOUG AIODB AVJOI DCANSOIDVN AOIVBNS
AFDJASDLFKAS JDLFKASD JFFASD JFALSDKFJ ASLDF
JASDLK FSJDLFK AJLGAKSDJFOWAIEFJAWOIRGNAI
AORINAFVNADKV ASDNVKA LDNVALSDV KASNF
LBKADFBN A IRNWOINWAEOAIWENFOW;AIEF-
NAOE IQPWOASJDLAS DVK ASKD ASDJVKAS
LDVJKASL DVJSALDV KJASDLVK ASJDVLK ASJVLSD
KFBJAROINEROBIE RNBIAR BANORI BNEOR
BNAORI BANRO WIANWROV AIWNV AWOVAN
IOVAOEVAI SDVAS KDVOQIEASLVNSDVLKANSIOVA
NSLD;VK ASLDVNA SKDLV ANSDLVK ASKDL
VAWIEFOWAIEFNAO;IWENAOWEIFJQIWE-
FAWEIFAWJEIFAOEJ EFIAJWE FIAW;EOFJ OAWEIFJ
EFI AIEF JAWOEIFJA WEIFAWEJOIAWEGJAW-
IGAW;ROGAJWOGIAWRGJAOWRIG WGIJARG
IAJBAKAS JVALSKFJ ASLDFKJASEJNWEFKJAN SGA
RGSD BD BGA GA ERHR TH SRGNAS GKNAROGA
WREIGNAROGIANRGO AIRG AORGN AOERIG
NAEROG NAROA RBOANR IFANROAIWNEFOAIE
NFOABN IEBORNEST IOAWRETIOAWEI RWET
ISOUG AIODB AVJOI DCANSOIDVN AOIVBNS
AFDJASDLFKAS JDLFKASD JFFASD JFALSDKFJ ASLDF
JASDLK FSJDLFK AJLGAKSDJFOWAIEFJAWOIRGNAI
AORINAFVNADKV ASDNVKA LDNVALSDV KASNF
LBKADFBN A IRNWOINWAEOAIWENFOW;AIEF-
NAOE IQPWOASJDLAS DVK ASKD ASDJVKAS
LDVJKASL DVJSALDV KJASDLVK ASJDVLK ASJVLSD
KFBJAROINEROBIE RNBIAR BANORI BNEOR
BNAORI BANRO WIANWROV AIWNV AWOVAN
IOVAOEVAI SDVAS KDVOQIEASLVNSDVLKANSIOVA
NSLD;VK ASLDVNA SKDLV ANSDLVK ASKDL
VAWIEFOWAIEFNAO;IWENAOWEIFJQIWE-
FAWEIFAWJEIFAOEJ EFIAJWE FIAW;EOFJ OAWEIFJ
EFI AIEF JAWOEIFJA WEIFAWEJOIAWEGJAW-

IGAW;ROGAJWOGIAWRGJAOWRIG WGIJARG
IAJBAKAS JVALSKFJ ASLDFKJASEJNWEFKJAN SGA
RGSD BD BGA GA ERHR TH SRGNAS GKNAROGA
WREIGNAROGIANRGO AIRG AORGN AOERIG
NAEROG NAROA RBOANR IFANROAIWNEFOAIE
NFOABN IEBORNEST IOAWRETIOAWEI RWET
ISOUG AIODB AVJOI DCANSOIDVN AOIVBNS
DFBOIAFDN O;IFB ANOSBFIAN SOIREN AERIOA
SE;FIAOS GNIAOSEFIN ASOIR; RIEAUADJFKASLJFAL-
SJEIEFAEBKANBKALSDK ADJFSKD JDK FJ DFSDKJ
FLWKE FJWEK FWJEK WLEJF KLWE FJK
JEFWIEORQUEIORUE W BKDNFVKDFNDKLFBNS-
DLKFNB KFKWENF WEKN WEFKWEFNALEKN-
FWEKLFNWELKFWNEKFNW EF
WKEFNWLEFKNWEKLFNWE FKWLE FKLW EFWK
ELKW EFKLWE KFLWE FKWNELKFNWELFK-
WNGLAKRGN KLNGERGNSJNSJKRNNKJASNFLQK-
WNQLKWEJQWLK QW J QWJQLKWJQLWK EQW
LQW JQLW KQLWJ QLKWJ LK JLKJLSKJSLDKBN-
BVLXNBLXKCBNLCKBNDLK WLEKFNWEKFWLNEK-
FLWENFKWLEFNKWELF AFDJASDLFKAS JDLFKASD
JFFASD JFALSDKFJ ASLDF JASDLK FSJDLFK AJLGAKS-
DJFOWAIEFJAWOIRGNAI AORINAFVNADKV
ASDNVKA LDNVALSDV KASNF LBKADFBN A
IRNWOINWAEOAIWENFOW;AIEFNAOE
IQPWOASJDLAS DVK ASKD ASDJVKAS LDVJKASL
DVJSALDV KJASDLVK ASJDVLK ASJVLSD
KFBJAROINEROBIE RNBIAR BANORI BNEOR
BNAORI BANRO WIANWROV AIWNV AWOVAN
IOVAOEVAI SDVAS KDVOQIEASLVNSDVLKANSIOVA
NSLD;VK ASLDVNA SKDLV ANSDLVK ASKDL
VAWIEFOWAIEFNAO;IWENAOWEIFJQIWE-
FAWEIFAWJEIFAOEJ EFIAJWE FIAW;EOFJ OAWEIFJ
EFI AIEF JAWOEIFJA WEIFAWEJOIAWEGJAW-
IGAW;ROGAJWOGIAWRGJAOWRIG WGIJARG
IAJBAKAS JVALSKFJ ASLDFKJASEJNWEFKJAN SGA

RGSD BD BGA GA ERHR TH SRGNAS GKNAROGA
WREIGNAROGIANRGO AIRG AORGN AOERIG
NAEROG NAROA RBOANR IFANROAIWNEFOAIE
NFOABN IEBORNEST IOAWRETIOAWEI RWET
ISOUG AIODB AVJOI DCANSOIDVN AOIVBNS
AFDJASDLFKAS JDLFKASD JFFASD JFALSDKFJ ASLDF
JASDLK FSJDLFK AJLGAKSDJFOWAIEFJAWOIRGNAI
AORINAFVNADKV ASDNVKA LDNVALSDV KASNF
LBKADFBN A IRNWOINWAEOAIWENFOW;AIEF-
NAOE IQPWOASJDLAS DVK ASKD ASDJVKAS
LDVJKASL DVJSALDV KJASDLVK ASJDVLK ASJVLSD
KFBJAROINEROBIE RNBIAR BANORI BNEOR
BNAORI BANRO WIANWROV AIWNV AWOVAN
IOVAOEVAI SDVAS KDVOQIEASLVNSDVLKANSIOVA
NSLD;VK ASLDVNA SKDLV ANSDLVK ASKDL
VAWIEFOWAIEFNAO;IWENAOWEIFJQIWE-
FAWEIFAWJEIFAOEJ EFIAJWE FIAW;EOFJ OAWEIFJ
EFI AIEF JAWOEIFJA WEIFAWEJOIAWEGJAW-
IGAW;ROGAJWOGIAWRGJAOWRIG WGIJARG
IAJBAKAS JVALSKFJ ASLDFKJASEJNWEFKJAN SGA
RGSD BD BGA GA ERHR TH SRGNAS GKNAROGA
WREIGNAROGIANRGO AIRG AORGN AOERIG
NAEROG NAROA RBOANR IFANROAIWNEFOAIE
NFOABN IEBORNEST IOAWRETIOAWEI RWET
ISOUG AIODB AVJOI DCANSOIDVN AOIVBNS
AFDJASDLFKAS JDLFKASD JFFASD JFALSDKFJ ASLDF
JASDLK FSJDLFK AJLGAKSDJFOWAIEFJAWOIRGNAI
AORINAFVNADKV ASDNVKA LDNVALSDV KASNF
LBKADFBN A IRNWOINWAEOAIWENFOW;AIEF-
NAOE IQPWOASJDLAS DVK ASKD ASDJVKAS
LDVJKASL DVJSALDV KJASDLVK ASJDVLK ASJVLSD
KFBJAROINEROBIE RNBIAR BANORI BNEOR
BNAORI BANRO WIANWROV AIWNV AWOVAN
IOVAOEVAI SDVAS KDVOQIEASLVNSDVLKANSIOVA
NSLD;VK ASLDVNA SKDLV ANSDLVK ASKDL
VAWIEFOWAIEFNAO;IWENAOWEIFJQIWE-

FAWEIFAWJEIFAOEJ EFIAJWE FIAW;EOFJ OAWEIFJ
EFI AIEF JAWOEIFJA WEIFAWEJOIAWEGJAW-
IGAW;ROGAJWOGIAWRGJAOWRIG WGIJARG
IAJBAKAS JVALSKFJ ASLDFKJASEJNWEFKJAN SGA
RGSD BD BGA GA ERHR TH SRGNAS GKNAROGA
WREIGNAROGIANRGO AIRG AORGN AOERIG
NAEROG NAROA RBOANR IFANROAIWNEFOAIE
NFOABN IEBORNEST IOAWRETIOAWEI RWET
ISOUG AIODB AVJOI DCANSOIDVN AOIVBNS
AFDJASDLFKAS JDLFKASD JFFASD JFALSDKFJ ASLDF
JASDLK FSJDLFK AJLGAKSDJFOWAIEFJAWOIRGNAI
AORINAFVNADKV ASDNVKA LDNVALSDV KASNF
LBKADFBN A IRNWOINWAEOAIWENFOW;AIEF-
NAOE IQPWOASJDLAS DVK ASKD ASDJVKAS
LDVJKASL DVJSALDV KJASDLVK ASJDVLK ASJVLSD
KFBJAROINEROBIE RNBIAR BANORI BNEOR
BNAORI BANRO WIANWROV AIWNV AWOVAN
IOVAOEVAI SDVAS KDVOQIEASLVNSDVLKANSIOVA
NSLD;VK ASLDVNA SKDLV ANSDLVK ASKDL
VAWIEFOWAIEFNAO;IWENAOWEIFJQIWE-

FAWEIFAWJEIFAOEJ EFIAJWE FIAW;EOFJ OAWEIFJ
EFI AIEF JAWOEIFJA WEIFAWEJOIAWEGJAW-
IGAW;ROGAJWOGIAWRGJAOWRIG WGIJARG
IAJBAKAS JVALSKFJ ASLDFKJASEJNWEFKJAN SGA
RGSD BD BGA GA ERHR TH SRGNAS GKNAROGA
WREIGNAROGIANRGO AIRG AORGN AOERIG
NAEROG NAROA RBOANR IFANROAIWNEFOAIE
NFOABN IEBORNEST IOAWRETIOAWEI RWET
ISOUG AIODB AVJOI DCANSOIDVN AOIVBNS
AFDJASDLFKAS JDLFKASD JFFASD JFALSDKFJ ASLDF
JASDLK FSJDLFK AJLGAKSDJFOWAIEFJAWOIRGNAI
AORINAFVNADKV ASDNVKA LDNVALSDV KASNF
LBKADFBN A IRNWOINWAEOAIWENFOW;AIEF-
NAOE IQPWOASJDLAS DVK ASKD ASDJVKAS
LDVJKASL DVJSALDV KJASDLVK ASJDVLK ASJVLSD
KFBJAROINEROBIE RNBIAR BANORI BNEOR

BNAORI BANRO WIANWROV AIWNV AWOVAN IOVAOEVAI SDVAS. Their tongues intertwined like two hungry serpents and their breathing intensified with the heat from the roaring fire next to them. Diane and Paco were so lost in the moment, they had no idea that Diane's husband, Chip, had just walked through the front door after working another double shift at Best Buy. The evening was about to turn deadly.

REFLECTIONS

*T*rying to stay cool in the Mississippi heat, Mr. George Clemmons adjusted his straw hat and put another pinch of Red Man in his cheek. The humidity was thick and, at the age of 93, all Mr. Clemmons wanted to do was sit in the shady corner of his porch and reflect on the long, truly remarkable life he'd lived.

Hand Mr. Clemmons a freshly squeezed lemonade with two fingers of Jack Daniels and you'd have the pleasure of hearing one amazing story after another.

Known to his family and friends as "Juji," Mr. Clemmons was born in the small town of Utica, Mississippi.

At the age of 4, Juji was already doing complex math problems. By the time he got to first grade, his teacher had him doing math courses normally reserved for students three times his age.

Juji excelled in athletics as well. When he was 12, he made a half court basket for the varsity team that won the state championship. To this day, he's the only high school basketball player in Mississippi to have led the state in scoring all four years of his high school career.

After high school, he studied medicine at Harvard and

routinely had his theories and discoveries featured in all the top medical journals.

Following his time at Harvard, Juji became an airplane in the Korean War. No, not a pilot of an airplane. An actual airplane. He was responsible for a lot of important kills.

In the early 1960s, Juji was a shark. He mainly hung out in the Indian Ocean. Many fish were terrified of him.

From 1971 to 1978, Juji was baseball superstar Reggie Jackson's helmet. Together, the two of them accounted for a whopping 240 homeruns.

For most of the 1980s, Juji was the middle C key on Elton John's piano. He was used by Elton to play *Honky Cat* approximately 218 times.

As he entered his twilight years in the 1990s, Juji volunteered as an activities coordinator at his local community center. Kids often asked him to be on their kickball team but he'd typically decline.

He officially retired three years ago when he turned 90.

Sitting on his porch, Juji spit out some tobacco juice and sighed deeply. He gazed out at the beautiful Magnolia tree blooming in his yard.

A slight smile appeared as Juji thought to himself, "What a life. What a remarkable life I have lived."

STAND-UP COMEDY

"*Y*ou know the thing that really kills me?" said the fruit bat, during his stand-up routine at The Comedy Cave last night. "Sometimes literally, actually. It's the part about us always hanging upside down. I mean, am I the only one who is incredibly light-headed every single day of my life? I go to bed at night and I wake up in the morning and all the blood has completely rushed to my head. You know what I'm talking about. I head out for breakfast and my vision is as blurry as it's ever been. I'm not seeing straight and I'm thinking, 'Did I not get enough sleep last night? Did I sleep awkwardly on a nerve or something?' And then I remember, 'Oh, that's right. I'm a bat. And, for some reason, we willingly dangle from our legs like some medieval torture technique for most of our lives.' It makes no sense. Am I right? Hahaha. I see some heads nodding out there. And what's up with all this white privilege stuff?"

NEW PARENTS

*A*fter much difficulty in trying to conceive—compounded by an extremely rough pregnancy during which Janet was on bed rest for three months—the day finally arrived when the Hansens would welcome their new baby into the world.

Andy Hansen, a nervous wreck, paced the hallways when he wasn't in the room supporting his wife. He'd never done well in these types of situations and his anxiety was getting the best of him.

14 hours passed from the time they arrived at the hospital. Finally, Janet was able to push the baby out of the womb.

Excited, nervous and scared all at once, Andy and Janet watched as Dr. Young reached down under the sheet to catch the newborn. On his tippy toes, Andy was able to get a small glimpse of his child.

And it looked like a microwave.

In fact, it was a microwave.

Dr. Young stood there awkwardly, holding a GE microwave. The two new parents stared at each other in disbelief.

Andy was the first to speak.

"What ... is that?" he asked.

"Well," said Dr. Young, searching for words, "it appears to be your new child. Um, first let me double-check."

Dr. Young stuck his head back down toward the womb and felt around.

"Yeah, there's nothing else in there," he said.

Andy nearly fainted but braced himself on the headboard of the hospital bed.

"Doctor, have you ever seen anything like this before?" asked Janet.

Dr. Young thought to himself.

"A microwave?" he said. "Of course. They're great for heating up leftovers and making popcorn."

This attempt at humor didn't go over well with the new parents.

"Sorry," said Dr. Young. "No, I've never seen a woman give birth to a microwave before. No appliances, in fact. 27 years in the business and I've never seen one appliance of any kind exit the birth canal."

Janet and Andy stared at the newborn microwave in silence.

"There's that expression about having a bun in the oven," continued Dr. Young. "This time there's no oven and the bun is a...microwave. Obviously."

Janet began to cry. Andy was quick to console her. They quietly held each other, trying to understand this unprecedented event in their lives.

Dr. Young kept trying his best to help his patients.

"If we're ready to start looking at the bright side, I guess this means there won't be any of those typical sleepless nights for you that most new parents have to go through. And none of that stuff about trying to figure out what to say when your teenage kid is going through the awkward years. You'll save on college tuition. You can watch a burrito go from frozen to ready in 3 minutes."

"That's enough, Doc," said Andy. "I know you're just trying to help, but I think my wife and I simply need to be alone right now. You've been amazing through all of this. We need to collect our thoughts, though."

Dr. Young nodded as he walked toward the door.

"I completely understand," he said. "Take as much time as you need. You know, this is normally when I'd ask you if you'd like to cut the cord. But, in this case, I'd discourage you from doing that. Because if you cut the cord, your new child wouldn't function properly."

"Thank you, doctor," said Andy, as he turned to hold his wife against his chest.

"Because your child is a microwave," Dr. Young added.

Andy nodded.

"We understand."

OLD FRIENDS

*E*njoying the crisp spring morning, Maggie rejoined her friend, Joan, at their table outside the Morning Fuel coffee shop. Joan cupped her latte in her hands and took a satisfying sip.

"It's so great to see you, Maggie," said Joan.

Maggie laughed and took a drink of her chai latte. A little foam remained on her nose. She giggled again and dabbed it off with a napkin.

"I know," agreed Maggie. "How we let so much time pass between catch-ups is beyond me. I love hearing stories about your daughter. She sounds like a riot."

"Oh, she sure is," said Joan. "The way she torments our dog should probably upset me. But I end up laughing most of the time!"

There was a brief pause as both friends sipped their lattes. Joan used a fork to cut off a piece of her raspberry croissant.

"You want a bite of my croissant, by the way?"

Maggie shook her head.

"No, thanks," said Maggie. "Honestly, I decided last week it might be time for me to start eating a bit better. I even joined a gym yesterday. I'd love to be in better bathing suit shape for when Rick and I take our Hawaii trip in August."

"No kidding," said Joan. "I keep telling myself that I need to start being healthy. It's hard to get motivated. Of course, if you're getting back at it, maybe I should do it as well. We can encourage each other and keep one another accountable!"

Maggie couldn't contain her excitement.

"I think that's a great idea," she said. "That makes it so much better! Maybe we can even have a friendly challenge to see who can lose the most weight!"

"That's a perfect plan!" exclaimed Joan. "What do you think our target should be? Maybe the first one to lose 20 pounds gets a fancy dinner paid for by the other person! It seems like that'd be a fun motivator!"

Maggie was leaning under the table and it appeared that she didn't hear Joan.

"Maggie, don't you think that'd be a fun motivation?" asked Joan. "The whole dinner thing? Maybe a nice bottle of wine, too?"

Still hunched under the table, Maggie let out a bloodcurdling scream. Joan jumped up so fast, her chair fell over and her coffee cup shattered on the ground.

"MAGGIE!" screamed Joan.

With a loud grunt, Maggie sat up in her chair. A satisfied smile appeared as she set her severed leg on the table, spilling over her chai latte. Joan stared in horror.

"I believe this leg here weighs about 20 pounds," said Maggie, proudly, while gently setting a knife on her plate. "Looks like you owe me a delicious dinner!"

It took a few moments of disbelief before Joan could get any words out.

"Oh my gosh, Maggie," she said slowly. "You just cut off your left leg! You sure take friendly wagers seriously!"

Maggie repositioned her severed leg on the table so that the blood didn't get on the linens. She laughed.

"I can't disagree with that, Joan," said Maggie. "Getting back to the topic at hand, I do believe there's a little French place that just opened near Sunset Beach that I'd love to try."

"Well," said Joan. "Like I said, dinner's on me! Let's get rid of this severed leg and see how soon they can get us in! It's been so good seeing you today, Maggie."

"So good," Maggie replied.

When things calmed down a little bit, Joan went inside to get another croissant. The first one was a bit dry. Also, it had a smidge of blood on it from a friend she just doesn't see often enough.

CONTEMPORARY MATHEMATICS

*T*his is a math problem pulled from page 182 of *MATH: 2 + 2 = FUN,* a textbook with a fresh, contemporary twist written by Dr. James Linstrom of DePaul University.

Train A leaves Boston at 9:20 a.m. traveling at 45 MPH.

Train B leaves Chicago at 10:15 a.m. traveling at 51 MPH.

Train C leaves Philadelphia at 10:35 a.m. traveling at 56 MPH.

All three trains are heading toward New York, NY.

A few things to note:

Aboard Train A, there is a small section of the train that contains a coffin. It's a normal-sized coffin, but inside that coffin is a smaller coffin, then a smaller coffin, then a smaller coffin. It's a very Russian doll type of thing. Opening each coffin reveals a smaller coffin inside. Inside the smallest coffin, though, is a tiny velvet pouch. Inside this pouch there's a note that reads, "What? You were expecting another coffin?"

Aboard Train B, there is a married couple sitting in row

22. Both wear kimonos and have wooden shoes on their feet. Both eat their meal with chopsticks. Both sip tea. Both have origami creations on their tray. Both have a pair of nunchucks in their coat pocket. Neither person is Japanese. Nor do they have any familial ties to any type of Japanese heritage. Nor do they have any Japanese friends. In fact, the whole Japanese culture kind of weirds them out.

Aboard Train C, a man sits in a seat with his pet parrot in a cage on his lap. Every five minutes, the parrot says, "Polly want a cracker." The man's name is Polly, so he replies, "Yes, Polly *does* want a cracker," and he eats a cracker. The parrot is 14 years old and, because of this constant mix-up, has never been fed. Not a cracker, not anything. He is beginning to feel lethargic and a bit lightheaded.

Which train will arrive in New York first?

NO EXCUSES

"Hey, everybody. Hey, guys? Walt? Walt, can you hear me down there at the end of the bench? I just wanted to say something quick here. If you all don't mind gathering a little tighter. Thanks.

I wanted to apologize for dropping that fly ball. As you know, the timing of it is awful, since this loss means our GlowTech Design team won't make the softball playoffs for the first time in 11 years. Now, I've never really been one to make excuses. So, I won't start now. But, man, the sun couldn't have been more front and center in my eyes. I couldn't see a damned thing. I was following the flight of the ball from the moment the batter hit it, and then, suddenly, total eclipse. That's no excuse, though. I should've had it.

And, of course, you guys probably saw me tweak my knee a little bit when I slid into third during our rally in the fifth inning. Yep, the same knee I had ACL surgery on 10 years ago. I *really* doubt that had anything to do with me dropping that fly ball, but I can't help but think maybe, *maybe*, it came into play at that instant. Either physically or just mentally. Who knows, right? Sports are crazy like that. I'm sure it wasn't hurting enough to affect me catching that ball. I only have myself to blame there.

And, you know, there's the whole thing about how left field isn't really my natural position. If Laura hadn't face-planted into the fence going after that fly ball in the first inning, I would have been in right field, where I'm much more comfortable. It's just, you know, an entirely different view of the game and the batter. But whatever position you're playing, you still have to make plays. And I didn't do that.

And there's probably no point in me even mentioning how tough my divorce has been. You guys know that. After a while it takes a toll. Of course, I'm not saying that my failed marriage is the reason I dropped the ball—although it is certainly a distraction. Bottom line: I should've caught it. Whether or not my wife had an affair. I really should've caught it.

And, maybe I'm being ultrasensitive here, but did you guys hear about that woman in Atlanta whose 3-year-old child has been missing for a week? You have to feel for her, don't you? I know if that were me, I'd want to die. Stuff like that has a strong effect on me whether I'm at home, or work or playing in a silly softball game. I literally cannot stop thinking about it. I wouldn't be surprised if it was in my subconscious as I put my glove up to catch that ball. Regardless, you gotta block those things out.

Well, there's no point in beating this to death. Let's go get some beers. I just wanted to let you know I'm sorry for dropping that ball, and I have no interest in making excuses or even bringing up the idea that the horrific images of those poor otters covered in oil after the Exxon Valdez crisis still hit me at weird times, and, well, never mind. We'll get 'em next season."

WILLIAM

$\mathcal{W}$hen William was 19, he lost his arms in one of those I'm-going-to-grab-onto-a-moving-train-without-even-trying-at-all-to-run-next-to-it accidents. As of this writing, there are more than 742 such recorded cases in United States history.

After having his arms torn off, William was distraught. It took him a few days of wallowing in his apartment before mustering up the energy to go for a walk and get a bit of fresh air.

He went down his front steps and took a left. Mrs. Hawkins was in her front yard reworking her water feature. She waved hello to William and immediately recoiled after realizing her mistake. Instead of tearing into Mrs. Hawkins with profanity about his inability to wave back and throw her negative words about that worthless water feature, he took the high road and simply said, "Hi, Mrs. Hawkins."

A minute later, he walked past his friend, Chico. Chico wore his fitness outfit and excitedly tossed William a football. It bounced off his thigh and landed on the ground.

A couple blocks after that, William's friend, Scott, came out of the back of a U-Haul in a sweaty tank top and asked William, "Can you help carry my couch?" He quickly corrected himself and said, "I mean, can you Larry my pouch?" But it was already too late. Scott felt super bad about his mistake.

William simply kept his head down and quietly fumed to himself. He angrily kicked the ground. William reflected on what he'd do with his life now that his arms had been ripped off by a train. Life is difficult enough as is, he thought. And arms are important.

That's when he looked up at a telephone pole a few feet away from him. It had the normal flyers posted to it: guitar lessons, missing cats, etc. Then something caught his eye. One flyer, in big bold letters, read "Push Up Contest, November 12th. Winner receives $100." William again kicked the ground. But next to it was another flyer. This one read "Looking For Someone Who Has Had His Arms Ripped Off By A Train And Would Like Me To Install Secret Robotic Arms So That He Can Win This Push Up Contest And Take Home The $100 Prize."

William walked away, contemplating what kind of sandwich sounded good for lunch. He then thought back to that flyer he'd seen moments before. The last one, not the one about guitar lessons.

He thought a ton about it.

After some consideration, William ended up going through with the procedure.

On the night of the contest, William received some sideways glances. There were some buff guys and his slender size and stature certainly didn't compare. No one counted on William as the favorite.

When the gun went off, that opinion changed. Unlike those around him, William's pushups were fast and fluid. His nose would get within a ½ inch from the ground before his powerful arms again thrust him upward.

The other contestants tired and Landon Kringer, the pre-contest favorite, finally collapsed after 214 pushups. Exhausted, he looked in William's direction. William not only continued with his exquisite pushups, he effortlessly talked on speakerphone to his girlfriend who evidently was buying a chocolate covered banana at a nearby state fair. Kringer gasped because William wasn't even breaking a sweat. It appeared that this guy was in the greatest shape of anyone in the history of the world!

William won the $100.

He finally stopped after 51,847,311 pushups when his arms malfunctioned and began punching holes into the wall with great force.

However, no one was there to see it because by that point William had been doing pushups for three weeks. The crowd had all left a few days before when they got bored and the venue ran out of garlic fries.

GOOD OLE GARY

$\mathcal{O}$h, you know Gary, too?

That guy is freaking hilarious. I probably have at least a hundred stories about ole Gary.

Like that one time when we were on a business trip to Fresno. Some tech conference. And we hit up happy hour afterward at the hotel bar. Throwing back brews and onion rings like our gosh danged lives depended on it. Hot babes everywhere. And ole Gary, he turns to me and says loud enough for everyone to hear, "Hey, Jordan. When's our fight home tomorrow?" He said "fight" when he should've said "flight"! I was dying laughing so hard I couldn't even respond to that numbskull!

Another time we were attending a Stanford-USC football game. We were tailgating pretty hard. Gary brought a sixer of Coors Light and a footlong hoagie from Quiznos that we split in half. So we're knocking back these cold brews, watching these coeds walk past and I turn to Gary and say, "Hey Gary, what time does the game start?" And he burps and says, "I'm not sure." Gary wasn't even sure what time the game started! How hilarious is that?! For the record, the game started at 7:30 and we didn't even walk in the stadium until 7:36. Classic.

I can also remember the time Gary and I were playing

croquet in the park. Just laughing our faces off and swinging our mallets around. I'd brought a large bag of Tostitos and a 2-liter of Dr. Pepper. Wait. It was Diet Dr. Pepper. Right in the middle of this crazy time together, a 40-something gal came into view walking four dogs. I was glancing over at Gary because I just knew he'd say something. He totally had that twinkle in his eye. And, sure enough, when she got close to us, Gary hit a ball and said, "Whoa, it looks like you really love dogs." I about choked on my Tostitos chip. The comedic timing couldn't have been more perfect. For the record, it turned out not all the dogs were hers. She was a dog walker. I think her name was Jane. Maybe Beth. No, it was Jane.

I could go on but then we'd all be old and gray and wondering where the time went!

Oh! That reminds me of another memorable Gary line. One time, Gary looked down at his watch after we saw Grown Ups 2 in the theater for, like, the 15th time and he said, "Time flies."

DOES IT, GARY?! DOES TIME REALLY FLY?

Good ole Gary.

If that crazy sonofagun ever gets out of prison for vehicular manslaughter, I'm going to give him the biggest hug of all-time!

OBITUARY

 r. David Guhl died July 14, 2012, at the age of 45. He was born on February 8, 1968. Mr. Guhl earned a Bachelor's Degree in Apiculture Studies from Boise State University in 1989. Early on in his life, Mr. Guhl knew that he wanted to study bees in a close and intimate way. Inspired by the 1988 film, *Gorillas in The Mist*, Mr. Guhl wanted to understand bees the way the Sigourney Weaver character experienced the lives of apes in the African jungle.

In his years after graduation, Mr. Guhl spent most of his time raising money to support his project, "A to Bee". His goal with "A to Bee" was to spend five years living in seclusion with a hive of bees. He would delicately move a beehive from the outdoors into a controlled, indoor environment that mimicked their natural habitat. Here, he'd be able to sleep near the bees, study them and learn about them in the most intimate of ways.

In November 2011, Mr. Guhl finally received the funding he needed to start the project. On July 13, 2012, Mr. Guhl moved into his intricately created "A to Bee" room. 20 minutes into the project, Mr. Guhl, perturbed by the itchiness of his wool pants, decided to take them off and change into a pair of denim jeans. While removing his pants, he tripped and fell onto the massive beehive. He received approximately 378 bee stings and died in less than ten minutes. It should be noted that Mr. Guhl was allergic to bees.

Mr. Guhl isn't survived by anyone because he put all his time and effort into bees, making it impossible to raise a family or even talk to girls.

All donations should be made to The Lung Cancer Awareness Group of North America. You probably assumed the money would go to "A to Bee", but since no one would be dumb enough to live their life in an enclosed room with bees, what's the point?

A memorial service will be held this Saturday at First Covenant Church in Boise, ID.

THE CAPTAIN

*A*s the passengers of flight 683 got settled just after takeoff, they knew they had a long flight ahead of them. Seattle to Moscow is quite a trip, which is why many passengers were already pulling out their pillows, blankets, earplugs, neck pillows and eye masks—anything that would allow them to get a little sleep on this eleven-hour journey.

The familiar ding of the intercom sounded.

"Ladies and gentlemen, this is your captain speaking. I'm Captain Jim Summerville and I'm joined in the cockpit by First Officer Andy Jenkins. We have about a 10-hour, 43-minute flight ahead of us. So, get comfortable and enjoy what will hopefully be a smooth flight today. We'll be cruising at 35,000 feet most of the way. Thanks for choosing to fly with us."

Throughout the cabin, passengers opened up their books, flipped through the channels of the provided personal TVs, or simply closed their eyes so they could get some sleep.

A couple minutes later, the intercom ding sounded again.

"Ladies and gentlemen, this is Captain Summerville speaking again. I thought the view of Mt. Rainier from the right side of our plane was worth mentioning. So, take a look. And, again, thanks for flying with us today."

A handful of passengers took a peek at the scene the captain just mentioned. The sun was out and it really was quite an amazing view. One by one, the passengers went back to whatever they were doing before.

A few minutes passed. Then, the intercom ding sounded.

"Ladies and gentlemen, this is Captain Summerville again. For those that care, we're currently flying over Yakima. These were my old stomping grounds growing up. I went to Davis High School and ended up lettering in three sports."

There was quiet throughout the plane again as a few passengers gave each other glances about the captain's message.

Then, the intercom dinged again.

"I'm sure you're all curious," said Captain Summerville. "The sports were baseball, basketball and football."

Some of the passengers shook their heads, frustrated with the difficulty in being able to relax.

The intercom dinged again.

"The answer to your question right now is 'No'," said Captain Summerville. "I'm not wearing my letterman's jacket at this very moment. Is it hanging on a hook right next to me? Well, the answer to that question is a resounding 'Yes'. Lettering in three sports isn't small bones. I'm sure First Officer Jenkins knows what I'm talking about."

There was a brief pause before the intercom dinged again.

"This is your captain. It turns out First Officer Jenkins does not know what I'm talking about. I just checked. Enjoy the flight, everyone."

A low level of murmuring and angry chatter began throughout the cabin. In fact, the large woman in 22C threw her neck pillow to the ground because she was so upset. Even the flight attendants gave each other curious glances.

Again, the intercom dinged.

"I owe everyone an apology," said Captain Summerville. "In fact, I'm a little embarrassed. A little while ago, I mentioned we were flying over Yakima. It turns out I was wrong. It was actually Ellensburg. Ellensburg is near Yakima and has a similar climate. But one thing's for sure: I certainly didn't letter in three sports in Ellensburg. Because that was Yakima. I earned my letterman's jacket when I lived in Yakima. As I said."

There was another pause. Then the intercom dinged again.

"So where are we headed? Moscow?"

Mary Gibson, a 50-something lawyer from the Bay Area, was the person who initially unlatched the emergency exit door and jumped out of the plane to her death. Fourteen others willingly followed.

Despite the loss in cabin pressure and general unsteadiness of the plane, the intercom dinged again.

"When I think about Russia, space monkeys come to mind," said Captain Summerville. "They were the first to send monkeys to space, paving the way for all the space travel that followed. My most obvious question is whether or not they ever brought all of those monkeys back to Earth. Or is there a huge chimp colony on the moon somewhere? Are they up there giggling and setting out banana peels for the astronauts to slip on? Crazy chimps."

The remainder of the plane's passengers proceeded to all jump out, knowing full well they'd certainly die by doing so. The flight attendants jumped as well.

Despite having an entirely empty plane, the intercom dinged.

"Attention, everyone," said Captain Summerville. "This is your captain speaking. A buddy just sent me a funny text message in which he makes fun of my fantasy football team. And I want to send one of those little videos back of someone giving a silly face. Maybe Chandler from Friends. Now, first off, these little videos are called 'gifts', right? Where do I find these 'gifts' on my phone?"

First Officer Jenkins flung open the cockpit door and jumped out of the plane. He even leaped in the direction of one of the giant turbines to ensure that he'd have zero hope of living and possibly hearing Captain Summerville's voice at some point in the future.

The plane safely landed ten hours later in Moscow.

As he used the airport hose to spray off any carcass remains from the side of the plane, Captain Summerville affectionately looked down at his letterman's jacket that he was now wearing because of the cold.

"Three sports, man," he whispered to himself. "Three sports. You did it, Summerville."

UNWANTED CHILD

$\mathcal{W}$ith tears streaming down her face, Emily walked through the front doors of the clinic. Few decisions have an ending that feels so final. And even fewer can cause the type of guilt Emily was already feeling.

Emily scurried through the waiting room, trying to avoid eye contact with others her age who were making the same choice.

"It's up to me," she told herself. "This is what I want and it's how it should be."

This confidence was temporary, alternating between doubt and, already, remorse.

The nurse called her name and she walked back to a small, stale room. The doctor was a man in his 50s with kind eyes. He immediately helped her feel more at ease.

"Emily, how can I help you today?" the doctor asked.

"I'm here to get an abortion," she said, the words trembling on her lips.

"How far along are you?"

"Eight."

The doctor leaned back, hands behind his head.

"You're eight weeks pregnant?" he asked.

Emily shook her head.

"No. Not eight *weeks* pregnant. Eight *years*."

She gestured to her son sitting next to her.

"This is Jimmy," she said. "He's my 8-year-old son."

The doctor remained puzzled.

"Are you saying you'd like me to abort Jimmy?"

"Yes."

Jimmy stared at the *Highlights* magazine in his hands, unable to get very far with the crossword puzzle.

"Emily," the doctor whispered. "I can't abort an 8-year-old. No matter how one feels about abortion, killing an 8-year-old is murder, plain and simple. We just don't do that here."

Emily broke down crying. The stress of the day finally overcame her. She shook violently as tears flowed faster than ever before. After a couple minutes, Emily finally was able to speak again.

"Are you sure?"

The doctor pulled out a legal guidelines packet that he kept in the bottom drawer of his desk. He breezed over a couple paragraphs and then nodded to Emily.

"Yes, I'm totally sure," he said. "Definitely not on our approved list of procedures."

Unable to take it anymore, Emily leaned over, kissed Jimmy on the head and told him, "You'll always be my son." Then she left.

Jimmy continued to stare at the crossword puzzle. He pulled a melted Kit Kat bar out of his pocket and took a bite. Jimmy then made an off-color joke about one of the nurses and asked the doctor if they had Wi-Fi access.

Epilogue: Jimmy wasn't aborted that day. After spending six hours at the clinic, he ended up going home and having a nice spaghetti dinner with his mom, dad and younger sister. As years passed, there was plenty of leftover tension stemming from that day in the clinic. But Emily handled it the best way she knew how—and that was by pretending it never happened. She would make one last attempt during Jimmy's junior year at Gonzaga.

RESUME EXCERPT

$2$008–2009 Head Chef and Host of *Just Press Start*

Handled all cooking and hosting duties for *Just Press Start*, a television show on public-access aimed at helping beginner cooks. The focus of the program was specifically on the microwave. As a team, we wanted to use a medium most of our target was familiar with. While we struggled with ratings, we received compliments from a handful of people who said we were pioneers for trying to make a weekly hour-long show about microwaving meals.

To give an example, one episode was called "Exploring Italy." In this episode, we microwaved a Michelina's pasta, two Red Baron mini-pizzas, a mushroom and sausage Lean Pocket, and a Lean Cuisine three-meat deep-dish pizza. It all had such a Tuscan countryside feel to it.

One of the strengths of our program was how it effortlessly combined food-making with peaceful silence during those three to four minutes while the product was being microwaved. Most hosts would've tried to fill in that time with instructions or anecdotes, but I thought the hum of the microwave was enough. Did this silence sometimes turn into awkward silence? Of course, it did. Actually, quite often.

Critics of our show routinely pointed out that using a

microwave isn't really cooking. Or difficult. To that I asked: yes, but does it make for interesting TV? And the answer to that was clearly "no". Our program finally went off the air in August of 2009 when literally no one was watching our show. Oh, and also because someone snuck into the studio overnight and stole our only microwave.

MELON

When I was 8, Papa took me to the state fair for the first time. For someone my age, this world was completely foreign to me. I held his hand as he led me through an endless stream of cotton candy and taffy and Ferris wheels and games. Some of it startled me, but I loved all of it.

Most of all, though, I loved the carousel that sat in the middle of the fairgrounds.

From a hundred feet away, I saw the beautiful horses moving up and down and going around in a circle as the music played. I remember breaking free from my father's grip and racing over to get in line. It felt like I stood there for hours before it was my turn. Finally, the rope lifted up and we all sprinted toward what we thought was the best horse. I had no doubt in my mind which horse I wanted. It was a black horse with blue and orange colors flowing over its mane and saddle and tail.

I hopped on the horse and tightly gripped its neck. I immediately named the horse "Melon". The ride started and I was quickly taken to a different place. I remember laughing the entire time while I hugged Melon's neck and waved to Papa standing on the side. It was the happiest I'd ever been.

I ended up going on the carousel ride another three times

that afternoon and five times the following day. And, yes, each time I rode Melon.

For the next five or six years, my world revolved around the fair, this carousel and Melon. I went back every year and rode Melon for hours. Papa would often have to pry me off Melon's back because I loved riding her so much. I even wondered what it'd be like if Melon was a real horse and not attached to the brass pole. I imagined Melon and I running through the countryside, going faster and faster and faster.

Before I blew out the candles on my 14th birthday, Papa pulled me aside. He looked at me more seriously than he ever had.

"As you make your wish," he said. "It's important that what you picture in your mind is as specific as humanly possible to what you want to come true."

Though a little bit weirded out by this instruction, I nodded to him and then faced my birthday cake again. I closed my eyes, pictured Melon running through a majestic scene as a real horse and puckered my lips to blow out the candles. But just as I was about to blow, I opened my eyes in time to see a photo of grandma on the hutch. Nana was slumped in her wheelchair, blanket draped over her legs, with a gentle smile. I smiled back as I blew, and the 14 candles were extinguished.

I looked up at Papa and I could see a look of fear in his eyes—a fear that told me I messed up my birthday wish.

Because Papa rented a dunk tank and a clown, I became very distracted with birthday fun for the rest of the day. It wasn't until my head hit the pillow that I remembered Melon and my birthday wish again. After a brief moment of thinking that I'd done something wrong, I found a peaceful sleep and dozed off dreaming about my birthday party and, of course, Melon.

I awoke the next morning to Papa talking loudly on the phone.

"She what?" he asked. "She is? She did? Okay, we'll be down there as soon as possible."

Papa hung up and then quickly swung open my bedroom door.

"Katie, something's happened," he said, breathlessly. "We have to go."

I immediately popped out of bed and he told me where we were going: the county fairgrounds.

We drove in silence, Papa refusing to tell me what was going on. When we arrived, a fair administrator came running over to us.

"Are you Katie?" she asked.

I could only nod.

"Come with me," she said. "Something's happened to Melon."

Papa and I ran with her to the carousel.

I heard the clickety sound of the wheelchair before I saw it. Sure enough, around the corner came Melon, blanket over her lap, struggling with her hooves to turn the wheels on her wheelchair.

"So," Melon said with a high-pitched, whiny voice. "This was your gawl-damned birthday wish, was it? To put ole Melon in a wheelchair?"

I couldn't believe my eyes.

"Melon!" I exclaimed. "You can talk?"

She snorted.

"That's your takeaway from all this?" she asked. "That I can talk? Not that I went from a beautiful carousel ride that all the kids loved to a crippled grandma horse?"

I know I should've felt bad but there was my Melon, alive! Albeit in a very elderly state.

"Can I ask you a question, Katie?" said Melon. "Why couldn't you and your dad over there buck up enough cash to get your grandma an electric wheelchair? I can't get around with these hooves. You really screwed me over, Katie! Big time! You've ruined my life!"

I thought for a moment and then an idea hit me.

"Hey," I said. "How about this? For my next birthday, I'll make the wish again but this time I'll be sure to *really* focus on picturing you as a young, energetic horse."

She looked down and adjusted her blanket, hooves shaking with anger.

"So all I have to do is just sit here in this wheelchair for the next 364 days and hope that, at that time, you'll be able to concentrate enough while blowing out your birthday candles that I'll be able to walk around like a proper horse instead of sitting here in my old, smelly grandma filth?" Melon asked.

Not picking up on her sarcasm I said, "Yep!" then gave her a big hug and ran off to get a funnel cake.

SPELLING BEE

*B*elow is a list of words used in the 2017 Spelling Bee *Championship, along with the example given of how the word can be used in a sentence. It should be noted that the moderator, Mr. Doug Flynn, found out days before the event that his girlfriend recently cheated on him with an employee from Arby's.*

Chortle. "Even though the Arby's guy isn't funny, my ex-girlfriend let out a loud chortle whenever he said a joke."

Puckish. "Since my ex-girlfriend was puckish, you never knew what she was up to. I'll tell you what she was up to: getting a little Arby's sauce on the side, if you know what I mean. You know what I mean. Again, the word is 'puckish'."

Aficionado. "My ex-girlfriend was an aficionado, or a fan, of screwing me over mightily. If she thinks she's getting out of this without returning my Seattle Seahawks Jerry Rice jersey, she's sadly mistaken."

Irrefragable. "It's nearly irrefragable, or impossible, to say that my ex-girlfriend wasn't a dirty, dirty woman. Everyone thinks so. Even her family. Well, I texted her parents about it and I'm pretty confident they think she's dirty as well. 'Irrefragable' is the word."

Mellifluous. "She probably hooked up with some guy named Mellifluous as well. No clue if Mellifluous worked at Arby's."

Maudlin. "Same with Maudlin. She totally fooled around with him. Like I said, my ex was a real bimbo."

Coterminous. "Is Coterminous an STD? If so, I'm sure my ex-girlfriend has it."

Inebriated. "As soon as we've crowned the King Spelling Nerd at the end of the day, I'm going to go get myself a little bit inebriated. And maybe drunk dial my ex-girlfriend. Hopefully not. But I'm not making any guarantees. I really miss her. She's the best thing that's ever happened to me."

VETERINARIAN

*D*ear Mrs. Phillips,
  Below is a detailed report on the health of your Persian cat, Fluff. The report is based on the extensive exams we put Fluff through today and includes recommendations for how to treat Fluff as we move forward. As always, we thank you for trusting this important member of your family to Evergreen Animal Clinic.

Notes/Discoveries:

- You'll notice Fluff's front left leg has been removed. More on that later.
- We weren't necessarily able to put our finger on the reason why Fluff has been sneezing so much lately. Kitty colds are actually quite common. We recommend keeping an eye on him. If symptoms persist, we can certainly prescribe a very low-dose drug to see if that helps.
- As mentioned above, we took off Fluff's leg. The leg itself wasn't a problem—there was no infection or injury to speak of. We just thought that losing a

leg might distract Fluff from that little cold he has (see point #2 above). As humans, we all know how frustrating colds can be. And then pretend for a second that you're now a cat and you have that same cold. How awful!

- If this cold keeps up, please let us know and we'll prescribe the proper medication.
- At that future date, we'll also make the decision on whether or not another leg removal is necessary.

Thanks again.
    Your friends at E.A.C.

THE LONG CON

*T*ina was 7 when she felt someone scooch onto her school bus seat with her. She'd been looking out the window, watching the autumn colors blur past when she realized she had a visitor.

"Hi," said her new friend. "I'm Louie."

Tina was immediately smitten by Louie. He wore a backwards Brooklyn Dodgers cap and had one of those quirky smiles with a couple missing teeth.

"Hi," she said in return. "I'm Tina."

And like that the two became inseparable. They'd eat together, play at recess together, whisper in each other's ears and hold hands while walking around the neighborhood.

They remained together through high school. In fact, the high school sweethearts were voted in as the Homecoming King and Queen. Louie was the star quarterback and Tina was head cheerleader.

Louie and Tina got married soon after graduation. They stayed on at Louie's grandparents' farm, helped with chores and within five years they had their first child, Henry.

The grandparents eventually passed away and Louie, Tina and their six total children took over the farm. It was on this farm that Louie and Tina taught their kids right from wrong, how to be good, moral people, as well as reading, writing and arithmetic.

As kids do, they all grew up and moved away from that beautiful farm. It was okay with their parents as they were happy their children were able to spread their wings and explore all the world has to offer.

Louie and Tina grew old together. Very old.

They were both in their late 80s when, one day, they were drinking coffee in the breakfast nook. Tina had taken a few bites of an English muffin when she realized she had a few crumbs on her chin. She stood up slowly.

"I need to get a napkin, dear," said Tina. "I'll be right back."

She gave Louie a kiss on the forehead.

When Tina left the room, Louie looked around suspiciously. He even briefly peered out the window. Assured that the coast was clear, Louie took a deep breath. He then reached over to Tina's purse and found her billfold. Inside were two worn-out five-dollar bills. He took another quick look around before grabbing the ten dollars and stuffing them in his pocket.

Louie then stood up, snuck out the back door, and laughed maniacally as he got in his Cadillac and inched out of the driveway.

"I did it!" he exclaimed. "I finally did it! I conned her! Boy oh boy I conned her good! It only took 82 years but I got her money! Ten dollars! Ten dollars!!!"

Though he didn't notice her, Tina stood at the window and watched her husband gleefully drive away with her ten dollars. While she felt a bit duped, Louie had recently taken on the typical pungent, musty odor associated with many elderly people.

So, yes, she'd miss her swindling husband of 60 years. But at least the house might smell a little better.

HIGH SCHOOL CROSS COUNTRY COACH

*C*OACH: So, are you good at baseball, son? Any chance the baseball coach will try to swoop in and steal you away from me?

STUDENT: Nope.

COACH: Great. What about basketball? Any chance the basketball coach will be after you?

STUDENT: Nope.

COACH: Great. Soccer?

STUDENT: Nope.

COACH: Tennis?

STUDENT: Nope.

COACH: Football?

STUDENT: Nope.

COACH: Wrestling?

STUDENT: Nope.

COACH: Do you have any coordination or athletic talents whatsoever?

STUDENT: Not really.

COACH: Great. Welcome to the cross-country team. Here are some tiny lady shorts to change into.

THOREAU'S FIRST TRIP TO THE WOODS

*A*lifetime before *Walden*, Henry David Thoreau was still perfecting his writing craft. Below is a small collection of unpublished poems Thoreau—then known as "Hank"—wrote during a trip to the woods as a 19-year-old.

The Forest at Midnight

The evening sound awakens me.
I leave my tent and step onto the moonlit forest floor.
I must find the source.
Do my ears hear pain? Pleasure?
I smell the source before I see it.
A raccoon with diarrhea.
Hind legs quivering, the poor creature can only look at me, ashamed.
There's no end in sight.
I return to the tent and consider cutting off my ears with a utility knife.

Infinite Stream

The stream is endless.
Infinite movement.
No beginning and no ending.
Unless you count the lake it pours into about 50 meters from here.
So, yes, I suppose the stream does have an ending. I stand corrected.
Oh, look. Another fish.

Message From the Trees

If only the trees could speak.
If only they could impart century-old wisdom.
Guidance.
Strength.
Instead they simply stand there, chucking pine cones at me.

A View From Above

The hawk spreads its wings and soars.
Oh, to view life from a new perspective!
To look down from the skies above and see
humankind's movement.
Our efforts.
Our frailty.
The hawk swoops down.
Quickly.
Violently.
Is it after my sandwich?
Do hawks even like egg salad sandwiches?
I drop the sandwich and run.
Pee involuntarily leaves my body.

A Lesson in Patience

The world slows down in the woods.
In the nearby creek, a turtle sits on a log.
I watch it intently.
It rests peacefully.
How I yearn to find that contentment in my life.
An hour passes.
Two.
Three.
The turtle doesn't move a muscle.
Four hours pass.
Five.
I'm bored to tears.
I could've been hiking or bird watching.
What a waste.
I'll never have that time back.

Hammered

Moonshine! Moonshine!
You are the best!
Zippity-dippity-doo!

BOOK CLUB DISCUSSION QUESTIONS FOR *BEDTIME STORIES TO READ TO YOURSELF IF YOU LIKE DREAMING ABOUT STUPID THINGS*

1. So, the book. Discuss.

2. The story about the adult still covered in afterbirth was obviously symbolic about how childish nature remains engrained in all of us despite the pressure from society to act a certain way as we age. In what ways do you attempt to hold onto behaviors from your youth? Also, anybody in the book club still covered in afterbirth?

3. Without looking, what page number does the leaf-blowing story begin? Correct answers get a 10% off coupon to Sunglass Hut.

4. Because you're in a book club, you probably have a drinking problem. But who in the group would you say you're most worried about? Name names.

5. In 1988, Darryl Strawberry hit 39 homeruns, stole 29 bases and yet somehow finished second to Kirk Gibson in the NL MVP voting. Discuss.

6. There's that one pretty disgusting story in the book about the woman sawing off her leg to win a bet with her friend. Spoiler: it's even more repulsive when you read it a second time. Anyway, go ahead and list off all the different circumstances in which you'd gladly cut off your leg to get something in return. Thought starters: hot concert tickets, free oil change, etc.

7. How do you figure out who brings the snacks to book club every week? Alphabetical order? By height?

8. As is tradition for a first book, a single hair was plucked from the author's head and hidden somewhere between the pages in every book sold. You find it yet?

9. This will likely surprise you, but the majority of the stories in this book are actually fictional. Do you feel duped?

10. Seriously, who's hitting the bottle the hardest right now in book club?

11. What would you do for a Klondike Bar? Just between us, the author has committed second degree arson for one of those. Discuss.

12. You find that hair yet?

ABOUT THE AUTHOR

An advertising copywriter for many years in Seattle, Joe Gerlitz can often be found in the park, being fed by pigeons. You'd probably assume that he would be the one doing the feeding. However, it was on an unseasonably warm October day a few years ago that Joe finally tossed away his bag of food scraps and said, "Nope. Enough. It's my turn." On occasion, the pigeons will toss a nut or a half-eaten popcorn kernel his direction. But most days he returns home to his family, tired, hungry and humiliated.

OTHER NOTABLE WORKS BY THE AUTHOR